Check the back of this book for content warnings.

AF436601

PREYER CHAIN

Prey Without Ceasing, Volume 3

Andrew Franks

Published by Andrew Franks, 2023.

This is a work of fiction. Similarities to real people, places, or events are entirely coincidental.

PREYER CHAIN

First edition. October 31, 2023.

Copyright © 2023 Andrew Franks.

ISBN: 979-8223056676

Written by Andrew Franks.

Table of Contents

This book is dedicated to Greg Locke.

When I write a story I always strive to make it one you'll want to burn.

(READING ORDER)
PREY WITHOUT CEASING
THOUGHTS & PREYERS
PREYER CHAIN

1

———

If one more Christian says the word "context" at me I'm gonna ask Jesus out of my heart.

Does your church sell context lenses?

Will they correct my vision so I see the scriptures like you all do?

I WANT THAT.

I desire easier beliefs.

I would love the Bible to become so clear to me I can see through it. Maybe then I would feel more comfortable letting people know what they are doing wrong. I could focus less on myself.

For now, I see in a mirror dimly.

I search for a way to have faith like a child and at the same time give up my childish ways.

———

CHANGE (IN THE HOUSE OF GOD)
2022

Pastor Teddy Ross was ready for change. By the time the emergency meeting was concluded, he wished for nothing more than an alteration to the very fabric of his church and more importantly, his relationship with his daughter. He was wrestling with God to accomplish this. He also wrestled with scripture. At first it had felt wrong to question his beliefs, but now, he hadn't felt this spiritually alive in years.

"I'm not saying I agree with or condone *everything* we've discussed," Pastor Teddy shouted at a volume usually reserved for a main point in one of his Sunday morning sermons. "But I will say, I have started seeing things differently as of late."

"We don't negotiate with God's word!" one of the church deacons all but screamed. Four other deacons, two elders and the other pastors of the church sat around a big, wooden conference table circled by comfortable black chairs on rollers. The middle of the table's surface was enhanced by a wooden carving of Christ hanging on a cross. The conference room was large and well lit, with no windows by design. The meeting area was intended to be exclusive. By God's invitation only. It was often jokingly referred to as the *Holy of holies room.*

Some people were joking more than others when that phrase was coined.

Only church staff could enter the room. Many a serious conversation had happened here. Big decisions had been made. Last but not least, a plethora of gossiped words disguised as sincere prayer requests had been spoken around the wooden table in this *holy of holies.*

The man who had just screamed at the pastor about protecting the church's longstanding interpretation of the scriptures would previously have never lifted his voice when speaking to Pastor Teddy. He respected Teddy and his position far too much to do so—at least, he usually did. His name was Victor. He was the eldest of the elderly deacons, but not frail in the least. His gray hair and mustache were well trimmed and contrasted with his suntanned skin. He had been a founding member of the church. He had also attended the church that had burned down years ago on the very property in which this new church now stood.

Teddy knew just about everything about Victor. He knew the reason the man was so tanned was because he spent the majority of his retirement shirtless in his front yard, trying to win his neighborhood's best yard contest. He had won the last three years in a row. Teddy could tell by the degree Victor's skin had bronzed this summer that he was a shoo-in for trophy number four. He also knew about the skeletons in the deacon's closet. Over a decade ago, Victor had had an affair with one of the congregation members. God had forgiven him for that transgression, and so had his wife. The woman he had cheated with had left the church and was never heard from again. His position on the church board had been in question for some time after the indiscretion—still, he had never been asked to step down. Pastor Teddy had only been the associate pastor back then. He remembered the anonymous vote that had taken place to determine if Victor would stay in a position of leadership. Pastor Teddy's had been the only vote to remove Victor from the board. All the other votes were for Victor to stay. In this moment, Pastor Teddy desperately wanted to inform Victor that he had cast the anonymous removal vote all those years ago.

"But you do negotiate!" Pastor Teddy yelled. He slapped the wooden table in front of him, hard. Paper coffee cups upon its surface wobbled. Everyone grabbed at their cups so they wouldn't spill.

The pastor was a large man. He had been overweight for a while, but now he was more muscular than anything else. He had begun to work out after his wife had died of cancer. The workouts made him feel better, but at the same time he experienced guilt for improving himself only after his wife had passed. He was sure his thinking was off, but there was no stopping his brain from running amok when it got going. He was in his head *all the time.* He often thought that if others knew what he was thinking, he would be out of a job. This meeting was proving his theory correct.

"You all negotiate with the text!" He was sure that his head was turning red. He took a deep breath to calm himself and tugged at his beard. Messing with his beard was something he did when he was agitated. He was surprised he hadn't pulled *all* his chin hairs out yet. "I'm realizing now just how much I don't know. I'm waking up to the fact that I've let dogma skew my perceptions." The pastor leaned forward in his chair, wanting to make sure the next words he spoke would be taken with the highest level of gravitas. "But there is one thing I'm sure of. No matter if being homosexual is a sin or not, the way we've treated our gay brothers and sisters is a sin." He put a large hand to his chest. "And I'm going to do the work it takes, both externally and internally, to make sure this place rectifies that. From this point on, we welcome *all* in this church."

"But... but we already have an open door policy!" Victor protested. "You can attend this church if you're a homosexual. It's simply that they can't be in any sort of leadership until they change their ways!"

The others all nodded in agreement.

"Are you telling me," Victor continued, "that you would let a gay stand on the stage and sing on the worship team?"

The room fell silent, waiting for the pastor's response.

Pastor Teddy wanted to answer the question with something that would challenge them. A statement that was both heartfelt and profound. He thought for a moment, his hands pressed to his forehead.

I know exactly what to say, he thought.

He crossed his arms in front of his barrel chest and answered with an emphatic, "Yes!"

The conference room erupted with protestations and self-righteous guffaws. Many of the men stood and threw their hands up into the air.

Pastor Teddy remained seated with his arms crossed. He swiveled in his chair. A hint of a smile threatened to undermine his serious demeanor.

"No way," Victor cried. "Gays can attend, as long as they aren't throwing their sin in our faces. *They can attend*," he reiterated, "but *they cannot* be allowed to lead. Not while they are living in sin."

Teddy looked the old man straight in the face. "If they can't lead because they are in sin, then what's your excuse for why we let you stay on this board, Victor?"

The room fell silent once again. This time, everybody was waiting for Victor's response. He leaned back in his chair as if he had been punched in the face. The chair actually rolled backwards a bit. Every head was turned toward him.

"Now wait a minute!" he exclaimed. "Whatever indiscretions I've had are in the past."

Teddy knew he was referring to his affair that not everyone in the room knew about.

"I've repented and moved on. Whenever I find myself in sin, I ask for forgiveness. That's why I can remain as one of the leaders of this congregation."

Pastor Teddy placed his elbows on the table.

"Jesus said to go and sin no more," the pastor said, "not go and sin *some more*. Vic, I know about Darleen."

"That was over a decade ago!" Victor shouted. He stood and pointed a finger up as if he was an attorney objecting in court. "How dare you try and condemn me for my past sins that have been washed away by the blood of the lamb!"

"Did I say Darleen?" the pastor asked, his tone almost playful. "I meant to say Cynthia Turner. Doesn't her husband attend the same small group as you?"

Victor looked around at the other men in attendance, while somehow refraining from making eye contact.

"You've chased more women away from this church than the devil ever could have. And if I remain the pastor after today, I'm finally going to put a stop to it."

The deacon wore his guilt like a heavy choir robe. He spun back around and lashed out at the pastor.

"You're allowing your feelings for your *homo daughter* to persuade you to permit sin in this camp!"

A rage like Teddy never knew existed exploded in his chest. No, the rage was coming from somewhere even deeper than his bosom. It originated in his soul. It was like his very essence wanted to jump outside of himself and strangle the man. Somehow, he contained the explosion.

"Please," he said as calmly as he could manage, "everyone take your seats. We've heard from Victor, but what about the rest of you?" He pointed at a young gentleman wearing skinny jeans and a tight-fitting V-neck shirt. His hair was deep black and swept over to one side. A small tattoo that depicted a bird flying out of a birdcage adorned his forearm. He had attended the church since he was a kid, and now he served as the worship pastor. God had blessed him the gift of music.

"Chad. You're one of my daughter's oldest friends. Do you think Abby should be treated like a leper? Should she be shunned and kicked off the worship team for falling in love?"

"Falling in love... *with a woman*," Victor interjected. "Don't forget the part that makes it a sin!"

Pastor Teddy blinked hard.

"It's okay, Chad," he said to the boy. "You can be honest with me."

Chad looked down at the table. He was pushing his cuticles back with a guitar pick. Without looking up, he said, "No. She shouldn't. And actually, I've known about this for a while now. Please, don't be mad at me for not telling you, Pastor Teddy." He looked up sheepishly at the pastor.

Teddy was taken by surprise when a single tear rolled down his cheek and disappeared into his beard. It was a surprising tear of joy. It had been quite some time since he had felt the emotion.

"I'm not mad," he said. "I'm just so glad she has you as a friend."

"How long did you know and not disclose the information to us?" Victor asked, ruining the moment.

Chad shifted in his seat. "A few years ago, when we went to senior prom together. We were having so much fun. I was in love with her. I told her that I believed God wanted us to be together. It's... embarrassing to admit I said something so ridiculous." His cheeks turned red. "She rejected me. I was devastated. I think she told me that she was gay so I wouldn't feel so bad about being rejected."

"How did you respond to her revelation?" Pastor Teddy asked. He was genuinely curious, and not because he was snooping. He found himself hoping that Chad had received the news better than he had himself, initially.

"Looking back," Chad answered, "I took the news better than I'd have thought I would have. But I also wish I could go back and do it again. I should have been happy for her. I should have comforted her. Instead, she spent the night comforting me. Making sure I was okay with what she had told me." He looked around the room. "Abby was the first actual gay person I ever met. At least, that I know of. I was always a *love the sinner hate the sin* kinda Christian. But now I see things differently. I think this is just who she is. She's not sinning. If you knew her for real, you would know that."

"But the Bible is clear!" Victor screeched.

Chad shook his head. "Victor, the Bible is so clear to you that you can see through it. You're always looking through it and pointing at things other people should fix about themselves. Maybe view it as a mirror, for once. And when it comes to homosexuality, there are a lot of misconceptions about what the Bible actually says."

Pastor Teddy felt like standing up and shouting, *Hallelujah!* Instead, he nodded at the boy and smiled.

"Abomination!" Victor declared. "The Bible is clear. Your daughter is an abomination and the two of you are letting *wokeism* change you."

"It's called kindness," Chad said. He was usually a quiet man, only really able to display confidence when he was singing. In this moment, though, he might as well have been leading the church.

I would follow him, Pastor Teddy thought.

"Like the pastor," Chad continued, on a roll, "I'm obviously still trying to figure some things out. I pretty much popped out of my mother a Christian. I sometimes joke that I was born and then *born again* almost immediately. I've never felt comfortable questioning my beliefs. I always figured it was a sin to do so. But honestly, I've been questioning God a lot lately, and I feel our relationship has been more vibrant than ever because of it."

The worship pastor sat up straighter in his chair. "Abby is my friend. I support her. And if you want her off the worship team, you're going to have to kick me off it, too."

Grumbling sounded throughout the room. It was hard to tell if people were agreeing or disagreeing with Chad.

The only person whose opinion was obvious was Victor. "If you show *too much* kindness and patience to that sick group of people your daughter has thrown her lot in with, you're doing nothing but telling them that you and this church condone their wickedness."

Pastor Teddy rose from his seat at the head of the table. He was a tall man. People had to literally look up to him. He looked around the room at the people in his life that he had always trusted. People that he had always depended on, and they on him. He loved these people. He respected them and their opinions, even if they disagreed with him. But he respected his daughter more.

"Love, kindness, patience," he said. "These are fruits of the spirit." He looked Victor in the eyes. "I will not be told to withhold those fruits from the people that need them the most right now." The pastor opened his arms in a gesture that encompassed everyone present. "You have all followed me as I did my best to lead this flock in the direction I believed God was leading us in. I believe He is leading us in a *new* direction. It will be uncomfortable for many of us. But picking up your cross and following Christ isn't exactly meant to be comfortable. Starting immediately, I am going to be looking for ways to make our church more inclusive. This means everything from my daughter staying on the worship team to making this place more accessible to people with disabilities."

"Or we could just have more faith that God will heal those with disabilities," Victor spat out. "Ever considered that?"

Teddy pinched the bridge of his nose and shook his head.

"Listen, things might get messy for a bit around here as we navigate the unknown. But I for one am ready to step out in faith. If we start to sink, we know the one who walks on water."

He walked to the door of the conference room. Before he stepped out, he looked back and said, "I'm going to leave for a bit. Talk amongst yourselves and then vote. If you vote no, I'll step down as pastor. It's as simple as that." He paused momentarily, his emotions getting the best of him. "I love you all. I should have told you that more often."

———

A version of this actually happened. It plays differently every night when I dream about it.

— Abby

DALTON'S JOURNAL

There are people who are in the church, and then there are people who are IN the church.

I WAS IN THE CHURCH.

When I was a kid I believed the preacher MAN (who happened to be my father) wholeheartedly when he told me that God had called me to be a pastor. I was going to be special, unique, like a Jedi with a lightsaber Bible. Like Iron Man with a suit of armor forged from my favorite scripture passages.

Like a white savior.

All that I required now was a wife. Someone to be my helpmate and ministry partner. Because behind every *man* of God is a smoking hot, silent, submissive woman. Did I mention my future wife was gonna be hot? I couldn't wait to preach that fun fact to my congregation as many times as possible. She would feel so special even though I would be the one in the spotlight. Technically, she could never stand behind the pulpit in any official pastoral capacity (except to make announcements about the women's conference).

After all...

A woman should learn in quietness and full submission. I do not permit a woman to teach or to assume authority over a man; she must be quiet. For Adam was formed first, then Eve. And Adam was not the one deceived; it was the woman who was deceived and became a sinner. But women will be saved through childbearing—if they continue in faith, love and holiness with propriety. (1 Timothy 2:11-15)

My religious upbringing convinced me to treat women like goods that could be bartered for in God's general store. The lessons taught weren't always as obvious as a male pastor reading the above scripture from his position at the pulpit he was clutching, but they were there, and they were life-altering.

I'll never forget a Sunday school lesson I was taught when I was eleven. I was in an awkward phase where I felt too old for kids' church, but still too young for youth group. I now consider my entire religious experience my awkward phase.

As per usual, the boys and the girls had been split up into different rooms. Some random guy, I remember his face but not his name, read 1 Timothy

2:11-15 to the class. He then went on to explain that we men have an obligation to lead. He said that God has our future wife already picked out for us, and that Satan would use all the other women to try and derail God's plans for us.

There were no questions.

My young mind was certain that God primarily used mighty men. Women were created *for* men and they should, with very few exceptions, remain silent and submissive. Above all, they shouldn't preach.

Women belonged in the background, or more specifically, the nursery.

I would love to believe that if the children's pastor at the time, Uncle Marvin, had known what that man was teaching behind the closed door of that Sunday school classroom, he would have intervened. Uncle Marvin was a good man. He wasn't like the other pastors. But the wisdom that comes with age tells me that for as open-minded and honest as Uncle Marvin seemed to be compared to the other indoctrinated adults that raised me, he was still IN the church.

For every step you take back, you still never see the whole picture until the moment you step backwards off the cliff you didn't know was there.

Later that same Sunday, I was sitting in a large room full of stinky kids waiting for the adult service (or big church, as we liked to call it) to be over so their parents would come pick them up and they could go to lunch. The children's church workers were exhausted and out of ideas to entertain us, so, I was forced to watch a childish movie in which talking vegetables taught me the Holy Bible.

I do not permit a vegetable to teach or to assume authority over a man; it must be quiet.

I had a lot to unlearn. I still do.

I KISSED PURITY CULTURE GOODBYE
1993

The room was cold enough that when Esther exhaled she could see her breath. She imagined it was her soul escaping. She wanted to escape, too. The walls of the classroom were painted blue, like the ocean. A cartoon drawing of Noah's Ark floated in the middle of the wall behind the Sunday school teacher. Animals with grinning faces poked out of the big brown boat as if they were cognizant of how lucky they were to have been selected and spared from a world-altering flood. Or maybe they were smiling because they knew that later they would need to fuck enough to repopulate a planet? Noah was there. He appeared stoic, for a cartoon character. His hand rested upon the head of a lion with a big, golden mane. Fish with merry expressions on their unnatural-looking faces splashed around on the other walls.

Esther had attended Sunday school in this classroom every Sunday for the last two years. She had attended church every Sunday for basically her entire life. She was getting sick of it. Sick of this room. It was her purgatory. She would remain in this state of suffering until she paid the price all tweens in that limbo state between childhood and true teenage years pay. From where she was sitting, dreaming about the future and the possibility of escape, ninth grade looked like heaven. The blue walls closed in on her a bit more each Sunday. Her imagination added drowning people to them.

A *very* pregnant woman was teaching the class today. She was standing in front of the group of girls. An introduction to modesty was the theme.

Again? Esther thought.

The woman wore a long dress that would most likely have covered her ankles if her pregnant belly didn't claim so much of the material. Her ankles were swollen.

Esther had been introduced to modesty many times before today. She practiced it, but was bored with the subject. It was as if the church leaders talked about sex more than the people outside the church did, the ones who were supposedly having it all the time. She wouldn't even know the word *fornication* if it wasn't for Sunday school.

Esther pulled out a black Sharpie and started doodling on her arm. Today was a fidgety kind of day. She daydreamed about being anywhere other than where she was. Her calf muscles tightened as she leaned back, making the front legs of her metal chair rise into the air. Her feet followed the chair legs and left the floor. For a moment, the pit of her stomach was bottomless. The chair was perfectly balanced on its hind legs. She gripped the cold metal of her seat with her fingers and pushed her thumbs underneath her warm butt. For a few seconds, her imagination allowed her to leave. She walked a tightrope over Hell. Orange flames reached up for her from a pool of liquid-fire damnation. Her feet struggled to remain steady upon the tightrope that stretched out in front of her for eternity.

She lost her balance, and the chair's front legs came crashing back down onto the tile floor of the classroom. Noah's—or, God's—flood once again surrounded her. The painted water of the classroom walls doused the imaginary flames in her mind. She had preferred the flames.

"Esther!" the teacher shrieked.

The teacher's name was Hope. Esther didn't know *exactly* how old Hope was, but she did know that she was young. She was *very* young. Hope had graduated from Trussville Christian Academy last year. Esther was in eighth grade last year, and at Trussville, eighth graders and seniors sometimes had classes together as it was a small Christian school. Because of this, Esther knew something about the teacher that no one else in the Sunday school class was privy to. Today's lesson on modesty was being delivered by a woman who had given the church's music pastor a blowjob under the gymnasium bleachers.

The pastor hadn't been a pastor at the time. His name was Warren. He had graduated the year before Hope. Everyone loved Warren, including Esther. He had been the captain of the football team and, more importantly, the leader of the school's Bible club. The guy was *super* into prayer. It was his thing. Win or lose, he made his football team take a knee and pray on the field before and after every game. He would sometimes use the school's intercom system to ask the students to agree with him in prayer for something that the Lord had lain on his heart. As far as Esther knew, he was the only student that ever had access to the system.

Most importantly, he organized the school's *See you at the pole* student-led event, versions of which took place annually across the nation. Thousands of students would gather at their school's flagpole and pray publicly while their unchristian peers watched. It was a great way to know who wasn't saved and therefore who needed prayer. If you didn't show up at the pole, you were bad. It was that simple. Esther had participated every year, even when she was in Trussville Christian Elementary School, which was on the same campus as the middle and high school. It was technically all church property.

Warren always led the *See you at the pole* prayer. Sometimes, he even brought his acoustic guitar. His voice was angelic. Whenever he sang "How Great Thou Art," Esther would get chills. She was uncertain if it was the Spirit of the Lord that gave her goosebumps, or her crush on Warren.

In his senior year, Warren ended the *See you at the pole* event by telling everyone in attendance something God had told him.

"The Bible tells us to pray without ceasing. What does that even mean? I asked God that very question last night, during my quiet time. He answered me by giving me a challenge. From now on, I won't be seeing you at the pole once a year. No sir. I'll be seeing you at this pole every... single... morning."

Esther and every other kid in attendance had cheered. The adults had clapped. They all made promises that day to meet at the flagpole and pray before school every day. Not all of them followed through, but Warren kept his word, and so did Esther.

When Warren graduated, he didn't go off to college, so he continued his morning ritual at the pole. The rumor was that he had turned down a scholarship to play football so he could continue God's work in the community. Because of this, the school extended him an open invitation to be on campus whenever he pleased. He was like a local celebrity. There were even rumors going around that he was about to be hired by Trussville First Baptist as the music minister. The school was a ministry of the church, so it only made sense.

Esther was happy that Warren was still around, until the day she ran into him under the bleachers. She had just finished changing back into her school uniform in the locker room after PE class. Her least favorite part of gym was getting changed in the locker room. The things some of the other girls talked about were anything but Christian. Also, they were so open with their bodies. Esther still hadn't got used to it. It was like they had never been taught anything about modesty.

I guess you don't have to be a Christian to attend a Christian school.

That's what she had wanted to say to them. The statement burned in her mind. It rested on the tip of her tongue like a hot pepper she wanted to spit out, but she always swallowed it back down.

Esther had known the bare minimum about sex before her forays into the locker room. All she really knew was that sex was how babies were made and that it was a sin to do it before marriage. She now knew more about sex than she ever cared to. She had entertained the thought of telling a teacher about the dirty talk that took place, but she was afraid of getting lumped in with everyone else when the punishment inevitably came. Also, it wasn't all the girls. It was just a few of the *unsaved* ones. It wouldn't be fair to get *everyone* in trouble.

The situation was extremely uncomfortable. After PE class, Esther would often wait in silence for everyone else to change, biting her knuckles, a habit her parents said she had had since she was a baby. They told her that it was the first thing they had seen her do on the day they had adopted her. Esther had been born in Egypt, but she had no memory of anyplace other than Trussville, Florida.

When the bell rang and the other girls rushed to class, she would change back into her uniform as fast as possible. While she did this, she often imagined that she was Supergirl, changing into her superhero uniform as fast as Clark Kent could go into a phone booth and emerge as Superman. Once dressed, she would sprint to class. She had discovered that ducking and speed walking under the bleachers allowed her to bypass other students that liked to talk too much, and to get to her next class *just* in time. On this particular day, though, she would end up being late for class.

"Esther, please!" Warren had said while shoving his penis back into his pants. "I'm gonna be a pastor at our church. No one knows yet, but it's official. Music is the talent God gave me. I have to use it for *His* glory. *Please* don't tell."

Esther had stood in stunned silence. She felt dirty, as if she had been the one doing the sinful act herself.

Do I need to repent for seeing this? she wondered.

Warren zipped up his pants. Esther looked down at Hope. She was on her knees. The girl wiped her mouth with the back of her arm and then looked up timidly to meet Esther's eyes. She put her hands together in a prayer pose.

Is she praying to me?

Warren navigated his way slowly past the metal poles that formed the underside of the bleachers to approach Esther. He tucked his plaid, button up shirt into his pants as he moved. He banged his head on one of the poles. It looked like it hurt. If it did, he didn't let it show. When he was close enough, he placed a hand firmly on Esther's shoulder.

"Don't let the Devil win and stop God's calling on my life," he said. "It's up to you, Esther."

Esther was late for class that day. When the teacher asked why she was tardy, she gave no excuse.

Not long after the incident at the bleachers, Warren became Trussville Baptist's new music minister. He and Hope were married right after she graduated high school. According to everyone at the church, they were a powerhouse couple that God would use mightily. God had brought them together hastily because he wanted to use them to build His kingdom. It was part of God's plan.

For I know the plans I have for you, declares the Lord.

God wasn't done. Warren and Hope were blessed with love, joy, and a baby on the way. Esther had questions about the timing of it, but she kept quiet because she didn't want to be a gossip.

"Stop being such a distraction," Hope said, more sternly than necessary. Esther stopped dwelling on the past and rejoined the present. She blushed as the entire Sunday school class looked at her. She ignored them and stared directly at Hope's baby bump. She leaned back in her chair yet again.

I wonder how many pregnant women died in the flood?

"As I was saying before the Devil tried to use Esther to distract the class," the pastor's wife continued, "your purity is a gift you give to your husband."

She let out a labored breath. She was sweating profusely. Her feet spread a little wider apart as she prepared herself for a movement she did not seem to want to make. She bent over and reached for her gigantic purse that was on the floor, the action taking additional effort due to her impregnated state. Her hand dug around in the bag for a long time. She pulled out a bunch of things that she wasn't looking for, including the high heels she had taken off and put in her bag at the start of the class. Eventually, she found what she was looking for: a gray roll of duct tape. She tried to stand up, but appeared shaky. She put her hands on her knees to steady herself. Esther didn't like Hope, but she was about to move to help the poor woman when Hope finally managed to stand by herself. The class clapped for her. Esther joined in reluctantly.

"I can do all things," Hope joked.

She used a fingernail to scratch at the tape to find the edge of the roll. It took her a moment, but she finally yanked out a piece of gray tape about six inches long. The noise the tape made when it left the roll was loud, like thunder rolling in. She tore the piece of tape using her teeth.

"Can I have a volunteer?" she asked.

The hand of every girl in the room except for Esther shot into the air, as if the pastor's wife was a magician asking for someone to take part in a super-cool, death-defying magic trick.

"Mary, come on up here."

A girl that Esther had known for years stood and walked to the front of the class. Her dark brown pigtails bounced as she moved and she wore a large, red bow in her hair. Her dress matched her bow, which was bright red with white polka dots. It reminded Esther of a dress Minnie Mouse would have hanging in her closet.

All you're missing are the white gloves and two big ears!

Esther was ashamed that the taunt had even entered her mind.

Forgive me for thinking that, she said to God.

She bit her tongue. She had no right to be judgmental. About a year ago she had had a very similar fashion sense to Mary. There had been arguments about it, but her parents no longer dressed her. She was now more of a Converse and hoodie type of girl. She had no tattoos—yet. She wanted them desperately, though, a fact evidenced by the drawings on her forearms. She adored the way her marker designs looked against the backdrop of her dark, Middle Eastern skin. She was also very fond of drawing on the white parts of her shoes.

Mary stood next to Hope and smiled.

"Thank you for volunteering. You look beautiful today, by the way."

Mary blushed.

"Would you please hold out your left arm for me? With your palm up."

Mary did as she was asked. Her fingertips almost touched the teacher's belly. Hope took the piece of tape and placed it on Mary's forearm. The girl's face scrunched up in confusion.

"This tape represents your purity. Your purity is your purpose." Hope still held Mary's wrist in her left hand as she addressed the rest of the class. "God has a man already picked out for each one of you. Once you meet that man, you need to stick with him like this tape is stuck to Mary's arm."

Without warning, Hope ripped the tape from Mary's forearm. The class gasped. Mary looked down at her arm and screamed. Esther stood, then quickly sat back down and started biting at her knuckles.

"Being ripped away from God's calling on your life is painful," Hope said, loudly enough to be heard over Mary's crying. She still held the girl's wrist.

"The more it happens, the less likely you are to be able to stick to His perfect plan for your life. God created females to serve and love our husbands. One way we do that is with our purity. It's one of the ways we worship our creator. Now, can I have another volunteer?"

No one raised a hand.

"In order for you to understand what God is wanting to teach you today, I need at least one more volunteer. Jessica, how about you?"

Esther looked over at Jessica. She was shaking her head. Her eyes looked as round as the roll of tape.

"I'll do it," Esther said.

She stood and made her way slowly to the front of the class.

"It's okay," she said to Mary. "Go sit back down. I got this."

Mary sniffed and tried to get her crying under control.

"Are you sure?" she asked.

Esther winked at her.

Mary returned to her seat. Esther faced Hope and pulled the left sleeve of her hoodie back as far as it would go. Her Sharpie tattoo design was fully visible. It was an intricate pattern that covered most of her forearm.

"I worked hard on that," Esther told Hope. "Mostly while you were teaching."

Hope took the piece of tape and pressed it firmly onto Esther's forearm. Esther had expected her to ask if she was ready. She should have known better.

The tape was jerked from her skin. Heat that started at the crook of her arm travelled down to her wrist. Her fingertips tingled as if each of them had been pricked at the same time. She closed her eyes. Colors and drowning people danced in the darkness. She was nervous that when she opened her eyes and looked at her arm, she would find that a patch of skin was gone.

She forced her eyes open. There was still skin, but it was as red as the bow in Mary's hair. Her tattoo was still visible as well, but the black marker lines had faded.

"As you can see," Hope said, lifting Esther's arm for the class to gawk at the irritated skin, "not only was that painful, but it left an ugly mark. Each time you give your purity away, you become less and less attractive to your future husband."

It was clear that Hope was trying to suppress a grin. Esther clenched her jaw.

"Again," she said.

Hope stuck the tape back onto Esther's arm in the exact same place. Once again, without any warning, she wrenched it off. Esther grunted through the pain. It felt like sandpaper rubbed against a burn.

"Again," she said.

The teacher was happy to oblige.

"Again."

"Again."

"Again!"

There was still pain as the tape was torn from her flesh, but it lessened each time. The tape was losing its adhesion. Eventually, the piece of tape stopped sticking to Esther's arm.

"Thank you, Esther. You can return to your seat."

Esther pulled her sleeve back down over her forearm delicately. Her tattoo was now nothing more than a black marker smudge. She marched back to her seat with her head held high. She wanted her classmates to know she was okay. What they didn't know was that it was taking everything she had to hold back tears.

Hope held up the now useless length of tape for the class to examine.

"You see, girls," she said, "your purity is just like this tape. The more times you use it before you're married, the more it's tarnished. You lose what makes you useful and attractive to your future husband. The two of you won't have what it takes to stick together. Do you understand what I'm telling you, ladies?"

Esther watched as all the other girls nodded to show that they understood, even though she was pretty confident they had no clue.

She raised her hand. Her sweatshirt sleeve was moist, her blood soaking into it.

"Yes, Esther?" Hope said. Her eyes rolled slightly.

Esther lowered her hand and leaned back in her chair.

"What you're so ineloquently tiptoeing around saying is that we should save ourselves for marriage. As in, no sexy time before wedding bells. Am I right?"

Hope's face turned red. She tugged at the tight fabric of her dress that clung to her abdomen.

"Yes," she answered. "True love waits. That is God's perfect will. Now, if you would all bow your heads and close your eyes, we will pray. Pastor Warren has probably already begun the worship service in the sanctuary."

Every head bowed and every eye closed, except for Esther's.

"Dear heavenly Father," Hope began.

"Excuse me!" Esther interrupted, her bloody arm raised and waving.

Every head unbowed and every eye opened.

"I have another question."

"What is it, Esther?" Hope snapped.

"I was just wondering, are you in God's perfect will right now?"

"What do you mean?"

"What I mean is... did you wait for marriage?"

Hope became visibly uncomfortable, more so than she already was. She picked at her dress again. It looked like she was digging a pantyhose wedgie out of her ass.

"Of course I waited. Now, if you don't mind, I was trying to pray."

She bowed her head again.

"Dear heavenly Father..."

"So," Esther interrupted once again, "I guess *blowjobs* don't count?"

Everyone inhaled. The place fell silent. Hope began shaking.

Esther stood up. She was feeling bold. It felt good to finally say what she had been holding in for a long time. She had heard it said that silence is golden, but speaking up had made her feel like a gold medal was hanging around her neck.

"Well," she pressed, "don't just stand there like you've got a dick in your mouth. Say something."

Hope opened her mouth to respond, but then closed it. Her knees buckled a bit and she grabbed her protruding abdomen with both hands. Water spilled out from the bottom of her dress and flooded the floor around her swollen feet.

But women will be saved through childbearing.

Esther ended up being the one to run to the sanctuary of the church and get help. The service had indeed already begun. Pastor Warren was up on the stage with his acoustic guitar, singing a worship song. Esther ran down the middle aisle between the pews like someone trying to outrun disaster. Congregation members stopped their offbeat clapping and watched as she leapt onto the stage. The music stopped as Esther delivered her urgent, yet good news.

For unto us a child is born.

After watching the ambulance pull away from the church parking lot to take Hope and her husband to the hospital, Esther asked her parents if they could just go home.

"Why would we want to miss the rest of the service?" her dad asked. "I'm sure the preacher will have a lot to say after today's events."

Esther caressed her injured arm and lowered her gaze. She wanted to answer her father, but something inside of her felt like it was reaching out of her body and covering her mouth. Her parents turned and started to walk back into the church.

"Wait!"

They turned back toward Esther, their eyes widening. Esther's sleeve was rolled up to expose the bloody flesh on her forearm.

"Oh my God!" her mother exclaimed. She ran to Esther and pulled her into an embrace. As Esther melted into her mother's body, her crying increased. A gentle hand rested on her shoulder like a dove. She looked up to see the face of her father. His deep blue eyes held her, in an emotional sense, just as tightly as her mother was holding her physically.

They communicated with her. *Tell me,* each of them said. *I will believe you.*

That was the last Sunday that Esther or her family attended church for quite some time. Her arm eventually healed. The was no scar, except for the one it left on her spiritual psyche. For the rest of her teenage years, if she so much as drove by a church building, her arm would begin to itch. It was a painful reminder of the day she decided that although she still believed in God, organized religion wasn't for her.

Years later, she would meet a man who had similar scars on his psyche, and they would fall in love.

———————

The best way to explain it is to not.

I have cried more tears than I care to share with you.

I'm still a Christian, except for the days I'm an atheist.

On the days I have faith, it is stronger than ever, out of necessity.

On the days I don't, I feel more clear-headed than I should.

I'm told I must have never really loved Jesus.

I wonder if his church ever really loved me?

In spite of my occasional disbelief, I now care for humanity more deeply than ever before.

I guess some Jesus got stuck to the bottom of my shoe.

Blessed are the feet.

———————

ROCK THE UNIVERSE
2023

The aroma of sweat and beer mixed together was surprisingly comforting. The floor was sticky underneath the soles of Esther's black boots, which made a noise like they were glued to the floor as she tapped her feet to the beat of the rock music. In the early days of her relationship with Dalton, she would have been down front. Her favorite place had once been right in front of the stage, in the heart of the activity, screaming along with the lyrics that she knew by heart because she had helped write them. Moshing wasn't really a thing like it had been back in the day, when the band had played more 'underground' shows. The occasional pit did still happen, however. When it did, she took great pleasure in elbowing the chin of any man-child that didn't understand the difference between being lost in the music and being an asshole. Nowadays, though, she mostly hung back at the rear of whatever establishment Starfold was playing at, listening to the music while she drank.

She was proud of Dalton. They had been together for a long time now, and their love was still burning bright, much like the pyrotechnics that currently lit up the stage behind him.

It was time for his big guitar solo. She couldn't help but laugh: from where she stood, it looked like he was farting fireworks. When the solo ended and the over-the-top theatrics had burned out, Dalton glanced up from his guitar, toward the back of the crowded room where she stood. With all the lights in his face, he probably couldn't see her, but he knew she was there. He grinned and shook his head. His long, dark hair was shiny with sweat. It flung around his head as if he had been submerged in the ocean and was now surfacing with flair.

This last leg of the tour had been *very* successful. Esther didn't always go on tour with him. She had tagged along this time because the two of them were going to visit family when it was over. They also had some *other* business to take care of.

Tonight's show in Birmingham, Alabama was the last stop of the tour. Dalton had asked the band's manager to make sure the final show was in

Birmingham. It had been entirely too long since they had visited his mother and his brother James. James had four kids now, one of which they hadn't even met yet.

"The leader singer is so hot!" a random drunk woman screamed into Esther's ear.

Esther leaned back on the bar to create a little distance between herself and the inebriated fan. Her elbow bumped a can of Dr Pepper on the bar. The can fell and rolled over the edge of the counter. Esther caught it.

"I agree," she told the woman as she replaced the can. "I think he's rather attractive as well."

The woman was wearing a Starfold T-shirt. The shirt was black with the band name printed in bold letters. Above it was a design of a deer's decapitated and rotting head. The creature's antlers twisted together to form a crucifix above the deer's forehead. Last but not least, the body of a snake strangled the deer's neck like a living necklace. Esther loved the design. She had drawn it the same night that Dalton had finally trusted her enough to talk with her about his intense past in the church. She in turn had shared her story of religious trauma with him. That night they had made love for the first time. They had been in love ever since.

The music stopped. Esther's ears were ringing. They were always ringing. It had used to drive her crazy, but she barely even noticed it anymore, except when the world went suddenly quiet. The crowd cheered, chasing away the unwelcome noise in her head.

"Thank you, Birmingham! Good night."

The woman in the band shirt cheered and lifted two beers into the air, one bottle in each hand. After a few minutes of gawking at Dalton, she turned around and continued to talk to Esther.

"I'm gonna shoot my shot tonight," she said.

Esther casually pointed behind the woman. "Looks like it's your lucky night. He's headed this way."

The woman turned around so quickly that she almost tripped. Dalton was approaching, his eyes locked onto Esther's. He had almost reached her when the drunk woman did a speedy sidestep and blocked his way.

"Your show was a-*mazing*," she told Dalton.

"Thank you," he responded. "And thank you for coming tonight."

He went to step around her, but she blocked his way again. This time, she placed her hand on his chest.

"I bought you this beer. I bet you're thirsty after all that screaming."

The bottle of alcohol in her hand rested against his right pectoral muscle. He took a slight step back and pushed the bottle away as politely as possible.

"Thank you so much," he told her, "but I don't really like beer, and I need to be somewhere soon. Would you like me to sign something for you?"

The woman rolled her eyes. She pivoted and staggered away as if she was not only drunk, but also insulted.

"Would you like me to *sign* something?" Esther said in a mocking tone. She handed Dalton the can of Dr Pepper. "Pretty presumptuous of you, Mr. Rockstar."

Dalton cracked open the soda and downed the entire can. When he finished, he crushed it in his hand.

"Ahh. It burns so good," he said matter-of-factly. "And I'm sorry if I sounded like a douche, but I didn't know what to say to that woman."

"You're becoming what you hate," she joked.

Dalton chuckled and sat down at the bar. He patted the stool beside him as an invitation for her to sit next to him. Instead, she sat in his lap and wrapped her arms around his neck. His shirt was soaked with sweat. The moisture seeped into her own shirt where she leaned on him.

"You're gross."

"And you like it."

She leaned in to kiss him. Just before their lips made contact, he belched in her face. Without missing a beat, she grabbed his head and held it still, so that his face was directly in her line of fire. She belched an even louder, longer burp than his.

"Okay, okay," Dalton said, waving a hand in front of his nose to drive the smell away. "You win!"

He coughed a couple fake coughs, then pulled her in for a real kiss. The display of public affection was cut short by a timid voice.

"Ex... excuse me?"

Reluctantly, Esther pulled her lips away. A big man wearing the same type of Starfold shirt as the drunk woman stood a foot away. He held out a vinyl record.

"Um... Would you... sign this, please?"

Dalton smiled at the nervous fan.

"Sure, my friend." He patted at his wet shirt. "Do you have a pen?"

Esther stood up and handed Dalton a permanent marker.

"Here ya go. I've always got one handy." She winked. "For autograph emergencies." She leaned close to Dalton's ear and whispered, "You still have work to do." A line of fans was forming behind the man who was speaking to Dalton. "I'll be at the bar. Don't take too long."

Esther left him to his adoring fans. She pulled out her phone and started tending to her social media accounts. Dalton wasn't the only famous person in the relationship. It wasn't a competition, but in some ways she was more successful than him. She was living out her dream of being a tattoo artist. It was all she had wanted to do since she was a teenager. Now she owned her own shop. Her body was covered with art, including some amazing pieces done by the best in the business. She also had many sketchy-looking pieces that she and her friends new to the world of tattooing had created a long time ago, when they were all learning and practicing on each other. Her favorite piece was a picture of a dove with an olive branch in its mouth, which was tattooed onto her left forearm. It wasn't amazing. Actually, it was lackluster as far as tattoos went. Some would be embarrassed by it or even want to cover it with another image. Esther loved it. It reminded her of her dad. She knew that in the Bible, the dove represented the Holy Spirit. Her dad wasn't the Holy Spirit, but unless Jesus Christ decided to actually walk the earth again, he was the closest to a flesh-and-blood example of the spirit of God she would ever know.

Dalton was covered in ink as well. Most of it, Esther had created. That was how they met. He had come into the shop where she was working at and had asked if she could do coverups. He had an awful, big-nosed Jesus on his shoulder. He said he was sick of looking at it, and sick of it looking at him.

She covered ugly Jesus with a picture of a probe droid from *Star Wars*. They were both very pleased at how it turned out. It did the trick and covered the old tattoo, but, every once in a while, when looked at from just the right angle, Jesus' eyes peered out from within the droid.

"He's still in my heart," Dalton had joked at the time, "but thankfully he's not on my arm anymore."

For ten years, Esther had worked in various shops around Florida. When she finally bit the bullet and got on social media, she became a tattoo sensation almost overnight. Her talent, combined with lucky timing and her personality, propelled her to heights within the tattooing community that sometimes she felt she didn't fully deserve.

She spent the next thirty minutes sipping lukewarm beer at the bar, and sharing photos of tattoos she had recently done on her clients. She didn't have time to share every photo of every tattoo she ever did, but she tried to post as many of them as possible, because for some reason clients took it as a personal insult if she didn't. It was as if they thought that if she didn't post their tattoo, then the tattoo wasn't good, or something.

"Times sure have changed," she mumbled to herself. "Haven't they learned by now? Every tattoo I do is awesome."

"Who's the one becoming what they hate?" Dalton asked in a mocking tone as he plopped down onto the stool beside her.

"Ha. Ha."

Esther finished typing out a few hashtags, and then posted one last tattoo photo before shoving her phone into her pants pocket.

"You look exhausted, Dalton," she said as she caressed his cheek. "Are you sure you're up for tomorrow? Like, mentally up for it?"

Dalton turned away from her. He rested his elbows on the bar and put a hand on each side of his head as if he had a headache. Esther took a quick look around. There were still some people hanging out, but the venue was emptying fast.

"We've been waiting for three months," Dalton replied. "My dreams keep coming, and just like last time with the fake job interview we set up, *you're* going to be doing all the investigating."

"True," she agreed. "But you should really reconsider talking to James about what's going on. He would want to know. Maybe he would have a different opinion on the whole thing."

"No!" Dalton snapped. He slammed his fists on the bar, which shook. Bottles and shot glasses rattled.

The bartender looked over at them and started to approach, but Esther waved him away. "Thank you. I'm okay," she told him. "We're just talking."

The man gave her a look that said he was on standby if she needed him.

"I'm sorry," Dalton said. He rubbed aggressively at his temples. "I... I just get too emotional when it comes to protecting James. He has kids now. I don't want to get him involved."

"More like you're worried he won't believe you." She had tried to say it delicately, but it had come out sounding accusatory.

Dalton turned in his seat and grabbed both of Esther's hands.

"You're right. But if for some reason I'm right, this could be dangerous. I don't want James' kids to lose their father." He squeezed her hands. "Not like James and I lost ours."

Esther's heart clenched. The sensation reminded her of when her clients would tighten a muscle underneath their skin just as she pressed a needle full of ink into them. Dalton rarely mentioned his father anymore. Whenever he did, things always got serious.

Dalton's dad, Gary Folmer, had been a pastor. He had been arrested for possession of child pornography found in a fireproof safe under his desk. This had happened after his church had burned down in 1993. According to Dalton, his brother James' soul had been kidnapped by a demonic witch that had been pursuing his family for generations. Dalton claimed to have spent the night in his father's haunted church, battling the witch to save his brother. He had been successful in saving James, but the church had burned down in the process. This was what had resulted in the office safe containing the incriminating photos being found within the ashes of the church. His father's sins had found him out. When he was arrested, Dalton was proud of himself, and yet he had also blamed himself.

He *had* allowed himself to heal, but his past sometimes crept up on him and made him act squirrelly, like anyone might behave when a cop car rides your bumper for no reason. Gary had been released from prison four years ago, but Dalton had refused to speak to him. Esther had never met the man. She never wanted to.

"Dalton," she said with as much tenderness in her voice as she could muster, "we won't get James involved. We'll continue to look into this ourselves. I'm just saying, he only lives a few hours from here. He's a doctor. He would probably have a lot to say about your dreams, and the fact that this isn't just any old church we're investigating."

"That's exactly why I'm leaving him out of this," Dalton snapped. "And you better not have called him."

"I haven't!" she protested. It was true, but she knew he wouldn't believe her.

"I shouldn't have gotten you involved, either. This is my fight. I should have left you at home."

Looking past the fact that she was offended by him suggesting she should have been left at home like a pet, Esther composed herself and said, "As I was saying, this isn't any old church. This is the church they built on top of —"

He interrupted her, finishing her sentence. "On top of the one I burned to the ground."

He stood up, waving his arms as he spoke. "The church they built on top of my father's transgressions! I defeated evil that night. Now some new evil has risen to take its place. I know it, and it's *my* job to fight it."

Esther knew better than to disagree, but she did anyway. "No, Dalton. Do you even realize how you sound?" She stood to look him in the eyes. "The plan is not to fight. The plan is I go in there one more time and see if your theory holds any water. I'll ask a few more questions and then tell them I don't want the job. If I find even a shred of proof, I'm coming out and calling the cops. You aren't setting one foot in that place. I can't risk you losing it."

"The fact that pastor wants to hire you is proof enough for me. After the interview you gave, there's no way—"

Esther interrupted him. "Times have changed, Dalton I don't particularly like this Pastor Teddy guy, but I'm not sure he's the complete monster you think he is. At least, I don't think he's committed any crimes. He's just an asshole. And he's trying to change."

Dalton shook his head. "Trust me. Uncle Marvin has shown up in my dreams a few times lately. He was insinuating this Pastor Teddy guy is dangerous."

"Did he say that, exactly? Did he say, 'Dalton, it's your former children's pastor here, who also happens to be dead.'" She lowered her voice. "'I'm just popping into your dreams to make sure you're aware demons have taken over a church again. A demon-possessed pastor named Teddy is also doing something bad to women!'"

Dalton lowered his head.

Instantly, Esther felt terrible. She had gone too far. She trusted Dalton completely, but ever since he had woken up from sleep a little over a year ago, screaming about evil rising in his old church, she had worried about him. He had changed. He was distracted and always in his head. The vivid dreams wouldn't stop. He had eventually come to a decision regarding his nightmares: they were a sign. He was convinced that the nightmares pointed to resurrected evil that now roamed within the corridors of the mega-church that had been built on the old Palmwood church property.

Dalton's theory about why the demonic forces were back and what they were doing was genuinely insane. But it was just plausible enough for her to see why he believed it. Women had disappeared. She and Dalton had searched for them on social media, but had been unsuccessful in tracking down a single one. They were the reason she had agreed to Dalton's plan. Plus, he could be very convincing.

When it came down to it, though, she had to ask herself one question. Did she really believe the stories that Dalton and James had told her about their pasts? Yes, she believed their stories of spiritual abuse, but what did she make of their *other* stories? They were fantastical. James had told her how he had fought "the beast" from the Book of Revelation at a church summer camp, to save a bunch of children. Both brothers claimed to have fought "spiritual battles" that had somehow produced real-world consequences. Esther had said she believed them, but she also knew that even the brothers understood that it was technically all in their heads.

Who's to say the world in our minds is any less real than the world outside them? she wondered.

The thought made her shiver. For better or worse, she was with Dalton. She would do this one last thing, which would hopefully help him move past his pain once and for all.

THE INTERVIEW
THREE MONTHS AGO

Esther's forearm itched like hell as the car pulled into the entrance of the church. She clawed at the irritated patch of skin while staring out the passenger-side window.

"This place is unbelievable," she said.

"It is ridiculously big," Dalton responded. He steered his car around the building, toward the church parking lot.

Construction of Hillside Community Church had started in 1998. It had hosted its first service in March of the year 2000. The newly constructed sanctuary could seat three thousand people, and the facility occupied a twenty-five-acre piece of land. The exterior of the church looked more like a factory than a place of worship.

"It kinda looks like an Amazon warehouse," Esther commented.

"Yeah. It does. It also looks more rundown than I expected."

The car moved past a rock waterfall lacking any water. The church's logo was mounted in such a way that it would have been visible through the cascading water, if any water had been cascading. Unlit lamps were directed up at the logo.

"It would all be very impressive if it were actually working," Esther said.

"That's the gymnasium over there." Dalton pointed at a building with a transparent dome on top of it. "And over there, that's the Child Development Center."

"The what?"

"Daycare. When you have a church this large, everything has to have a fancy name. I bet the children's church is in that building as well."

Every boxlike building was connected. The place was one massive compound that seemed to go on forever. Eventually, they found the main parking lot, which was empty and enormous, with scattered, tall streetlights. Dalton parked the car in the closest parking space to the church. Even so, the car was still at least fifty yards away from its front doors.

"You ready?"

Esther put her phone camera in selfie mode and held it out so she could get a good look at herself. Her dark hair was full of volume and curls. She did her best to pull it back into a ponytail. No matter how much she tried, a few curls always escaped her grasp and fell into her face. She had gotten used to it, and even liked it.

Her makeup was a bit heavier than usual. She wore a black pantsuit with a dark burgundy top underneath. Her chest tattoos were visible. A rainbow pin that Esther often wore was pinned onto the lapel of her blazer. Dalton had insisted that she wear that particular pin as part of her outfit, though she had already planned on doing just that. The outfit was completed with a pair of open-toed heels.

"How do I look?"

"Perfect." Dalton answered. "You're gonna scare the shit out of him."

Esther removed her seatbelt. "Any last bits of advice? I've never gone undercover before."

Dalton scratched at his chin. "Just remember to push progressive views. Talk a lot about acceptance and living your truth. Be sure to mention how important you feel female voices are in the church."

"They *are* important!"

"Exactly like that. Between that and the rainbow pin, Pastor Teddy is going to hate you. He'll get all worked up. That's when he might slip up and say something incriminating."

Esther nodded.

As she was getting out of the car, Dalton said, "It really should be me going in there."

Esther turned to face him, scowling. "Forget it. It's me, or we give up on this entire crazy plan."

Dalton exhaled in frustration. "Fine. It's you. It's you."

Esther got out of the car and bent to peer back into it. "Wish me luck." Before Dalton had a chance to say anything, she slammed the door shut.

A few times over the years, she had thought about giving church another chance in her life. There were things she missed about being part of a community of like-minded believers. The mixed emotions she felt about her religious upbringing were confusing. Most of the time, it was easier to just not think about the past. Today, though, she would *have* to think about it.

More than that, she would need to channel a bit of her old self in order to be believable. If Dalton was right—and that was a big *if*—women's lives could depend on her exposing this pastor. She would need to be a good enough detective to get something on him that she could take to the cops.

She took a deep breath and started the long walk to the glass front doors of the church.

They were locked. She was about to give up and walk back to the car when she noticed a side door that looked like an emergency exit. It had been propped open with a small rock.

Did they do this for me?

She went inside, making sure to leave the door propped open behind her, and found herself in a massive foyer. The air was very cold. Its temperature made her think of her old Sunday-school classroom with the flood painted on the walls. She took a moment to look around. It was like she had stepped into a civic center. The floors were shiny concrete. There were several coffee bars and what looked like concession stand counters. Elegant couches were placed throughout the open area, each with an ornate wooden table before it. Large banners with pictures of beautiful people hung from the high ceiling. The people were all smiling and had incredibly white teeth. Messages—*Come as you are*, or *Welcome home*—were printed on each banner. Farther inside the building, Esther came to a long, curving hallway that stretched as far as she could see. Metal doors lined its walls.

"Anyone home?" she shouted. The only response was the echo of her own voice.

She decided to walk along the hallway and try to find someone. As she did so, she noticed that each door had a plaque above it. She read all the names out loud as she passed them. "Volunteer center. Youth group. Men's restroom. Women's restroom. Activities center. Kitchen. Cafeteria."

I'm getting my steps in today, she thought.

"Pastor's lounge. Nursery. Child development center. Nursing mothers' room. Sanctuary. Sanctuary. Sanctuary."

"Um... Just about all the rest of them say the same thing," a mousy voice said from behind her.

Esther's body tensed. She spun around to see a young woman who appeared to be in her early twenties.

"You startled me," Esther said, forcing laughter.

"Not as much as you startled me."

The girl had beautiful red hair and angelic white skin. She was wearing a black dress with a jean jacket over it. The jacket had pins and patches everywhere. Esther liked it.

"My name is Abby. I'm the pastor's dau… um… assistant." She looked around, as if making sure they were alone. "What are you doing here?"

"Hello, Abby," Esther said in the most upbeat manner she could manage. She held out her hand in greeting. "I'm Esther. It's great to meet you."

Abby shook her hand. "It's good to meet you too. Are you lost?"

"That obvious, huh? Could you take me to Pastor Teddy's office? I have an interview."

"What?" Abby's face scrunched up. Her jaw tightened. "Are you messing with me? Because it's not funny."

"Of course not!" Esther told her. "To be honest, I don't even really want the job. I just figured I would do the interview anyways. By the way, how long have you attended this church?"

"My entire life," Abby answered in a befuddled tone.

"So you know a lot about this place?"

Abby swiveled her head as if she was looking for hidden cameras or something.

"You could say that."

"Then let me ask you something, woman to woman. How accepting is this place to people like us?"

Abby took a step backwards. "What do you mean, people like us?"

"You know," Esther said. "Women. Does this church treat women with respect?"

"That's a complicated question," Abby answered. She touched her forehead as if she were puzzled by not just the question, but the entire conversation.

"It shouldn't be."

"I agree. Are you sure you're not a reporter? Or maybe you have a YouTube channel you're trying to grow? Or a podcast?"

"What?" Esther exclaimed. "No. I'm not a reporter or a podcaster. Like I said, I'm here for an interview." Technically, she wasn't lying, but she still felt bad for deceiving the woman. She had been about to ask Abby if any women had mysteriously disappeared from the congregation, but she was afraid of coming on too strong.

"I'm sorry. I didn't mean to insinuate that your church is sexist. If you'd just show me the way to the pastor's office, I'll get out of your hair."

Abby scratched her head.

"Whatever. Follow me. Just don't tell anyone you saw me, okay? I don't want to be a part of whatever you're up to. No one knows I still have keys."

It was Esther's turn to be confused. "Um... okay. I promise to not talk about you during my interview. Sound good?"

"Fine. Follow me."

Esther followed close behind Abby as she walked down the long hallway. Abby kept turning to watch Esther, as if she didn't trust her.

"They sure keep it cold in here, huh?" Esther commented. She had begun to shiver.

Abby didn't respond. She continued walking down the hall.

"How much farther?"

"Not much," Abby answered.

"I don't suppose it's a little warmer in the pastor's office?"

Abby acted as if she hadn't even heard the question.

The two women walked the rest of the way in silence. Esther's open-toed high heels clacked loudly against the concrete floor. The noise echoed, making it sound like far more than two people were traversing the corridor.

Eventually, they reached the end of the hall and approached a door that looked very different than the rest. It was made from dark wood and a cross was carved into it. The door hung from a track mounted on the wall. It looked heavy. Abby took a keyring from her jacket pocket and unlocked the door.

"It's through here," she said. She used two hands and what seemed all of her strength to slide the door out of the way. Esther wondered if she should have helped the poor woman.

Once through the door, Esther found herself in a waiting area not unlike one in a doctor's office. The floors were wooden and there was a reception desk with a computer on it. The walls were decorated with corny motivational posters, within frames that were way too nice-looking for their contents. The poster directly in front of her depicted a man climbing a tall mountain. The text just above the peak of the mountain read, *I can do all things through Christ, who strengthens me.* Underneath the office art was a large fish tank.

"Beautiful fish," Esther said.

"You like the fish?"

"They're wonderful." Esther pointed at a spotted gray fish that had its weird-looking mouth pressed against the glass as it feasted on the naturally occurring algae. "That one is my favorite. I've always had a thing for sucker fish."

Next to the fish tank was a comfortable-looking couch, much like the ones Esther had seen in the foyer. A large mirror hung above it.

Abby motioned toward the couch. "Make yourself at home," she said.

Esther sat down. Abby started to leave through the way they had come in, then paused as if something was nagging at her.

"Listen," she said, "this story is not worth it. Trust me."

"Is there something specific about this place you're trying to tell me?"

Abby let out a single "*Ha.*"

She took out her phone and messed with it for a second.

"There you go. Against my better judgment I just AirDropped you my contact info. When you don't find what you're looking for here, give me a call. Maybe I'll finally be ready to talk."

With that, she turned and walked away.

Almost immediately, the face of another woman peeked out from behind the computer monitor at the reception desk. She had beautiful blonde hair and a glowing smile.

She waved at Esther. "When did you get here?" she asked cheerfully. "I hope you haven't been waiting long."

"Oh, no worries. I just arrived. I'm here for my interview with Pastor Teddy."

"Wonderful. I'll let you know when he's ready for you, okay?"

She disappeared behind her computer screen.

Half an hour later, Esther was still sitting on the couch. She was also freezing, but there wasn't much she could do about it. She tried counting the fish in the fish tank. It was a difficult task, as they swam back and forth and hid within fluorescent rock structures. The church phone rang constantly. She wondered how the receptionist ever got any work done between answering calls.

Esther's cell phone buzzed, too. Dalton would not stop texting her. It was annoying.

Are you okay? his most recent text read.

So annoying.

My phone is almost dead, she texted back. Her fingers were so cold she could barely control what she was typing. She spelled words incorrectly, but thankfully the autocorrect took care of it. Three dots appeared as Dalton typed out a response. Her phone vibrated.

Abort. I have a bad feeling about this.

She didn't think typing out a response would be possible with her frozen fingers, so she switched off her phone and ignored him.

He's spiraling, she thought.

She stood and started walking around the waiting room to get her blood pumping. It was a relatively small area, but any movement was better than no movement. She entertained the thought of giving Dalton his wish and just leaving.

We really should just call this investigation off, she thought. *It would be the best thing for our mental health.*

"I c-can't b-believe I let it g-go this far," she said through chattering teeth as she continued to pace. After a few more laps around the waiting area, she stopped and looked at herself in the mirror.

"This whole thing is r-r-ridiculous," she watched herself say. "I'm g-g-getting out of here."

She started for the door.

"Would you like to wear my jacket?"

Esther paused.

"I'm so sorry. I should have offered it sooner."

Esther turned to see the receptionist walking toward her and taking off her jacket. She held it out in front of her. "Here. Take it."

Esther wanted to refuse the offer and leave, but before any words came out she had already taken the jacket and began to put it on.

"Th-thank you s-s-so mu-much," she struggled to say as she struggled to put on the jacket. It was more like a winter coat, big and fluffy and with a hood attached. She zipped the jacket up and threw on the hood without shame.

"Don't worry about it," the receptionist said.

"W-why do they keep it s-s-so cold?" Esther asked. "How do you have church with it l-l-like this?"

The woman reached out and rubbed Esther's arms in an attempt to warm her.

"On Sundays it isn't nearly this cold. When you get three thousand people in this place and have all the lights and equipment on, it gets toasty real fast. Plus, it's less expensive to just leave the air on all the time instead of trying to cool the place down just for services. At least, that's what I've been told."

"I g-guess that makes s-s-sense," Esther said, her teeth chattering. She had been thinking that Pastor Teddy must have been a complete asshole to want the air this cold all the time. She had misjudged him.

"My name is Brittany. What's yours?"

"I'm Esther."

"Well, nice to meet you, Esther. I *love* your tattoos. I was peeking at them from behind my computer."

Between the coat and Brittany rubbing her arms, Esther was starting to feel a little better.

"Thank you. I did a few of them myself."

"You tattoo people?"

"Yeah," Esther answered. "I actually own my own shop in Florida."

"Wow!" Brittany said. "I've always wanted a tattoo. I've been thinking about getting the words *dearly beloved* tattooed on my forearm in cursive. Could you do that?"

Esther wanted to explain to her how stupid that sounded. Instead, she said, "Totally."

"I also thought about getting the word *worship* tattooed on my arm to remind myself to worship God at all times. *Not* just during worship services. You know what I mean? Like how we should live a lifestyle of worship unto Christ. You know how the Bible tells us to *pray without ceasing*? Well, I figure why not *worship without ceasing* as well. You know what I mean? Like when I offered you my coat. That was totally an act of worship."

Suddenly, Esther wanted to take a step back and create some distance between her and the receptionist. She was coming on a little too strong in the religious department for Esther's tastes.

"I was over there behind my desk praying for like, thirty minutes. I kept asking God if I should give you my coat. A minute ago I heard the voice of the Lord say, 'as ye have done it unto the least of these my brethren, ye have done it unto me.' So now you have a coat. I'm storing my treasures in Heaven!"

"At some point, though, don't you have enough treasure?" Esther joked. "I mean, you're already in Heaven... am I right? Why do I need all that treasure?"

The woman stared at her blankly.

"I'm joking," Esther told her.

"Oh my gosh," Brittany exclaimed. Then she laughed hysterically. "You are too funny! You gotta use that joke in a sermon one day if you get hired."

"Will do."

Brittany was still laughing. "By the way," she said through a giggle. "Why do you want to be a pastor if you're already a tattoo artist?"

Esther searched her brain for an answer. *Idiot*, she thought. *I have to start acting the part.*

She took a breath and tried to look as serious as possible. "I've been running from my calling for far too long. I'm ready to stop running."

"Amen to that!" Brittany all but yelled. "I actually have a calling myself. I want to be a worship pastor here one day. But first I have to—"

The phone rang.

Thank God, Esther thought.

"Speaking of calls," Brittany said with a smirk, "I bet that's the pastor saying he's ready for you."

She darted behind her desk and answered the phone on the third ring.

"Yes, sir? I'm sorry, sir. I wasn't behind my desk. I apologize, sir. Yes, she's still here. Yes, sir. I'll send her back immediately."

She hung up the phone. "You can go on back. He's ready for you."

Esther took off the woman's coat and placed it on her desk.

"Oh, you can hold onto that if you like."

"That's okay," Esther said. She began walking toward the pastor's office. "It was nice meeting you, Brittany."

Just before she entered the office, Brittany called out, "Hey!"

Esther turned to face her.

"I'm rooting for you," Brittany said as she pulled her coat back on. "I haven't talked to anyone in a long time. It felt nice being seen."

Esther walked back to Brittany and hugged her. She wasn't really a hugger of strangers, but Brittany seemed to need it. Sometimes her tattoo clients tried to hug her after a session. It made sense—she and each of her clients were forced to be physically close to each other for long periods of time. Many times, clients would tell her very personal stories during their sessions. Esther would always make sure to actually listen. It was intimate in a weird way. For some reason, the hugging had always bothered Esther. It also bothered her that it bothered her. But standing here, hugging this stranger, felt right.

"You better get in there," Brittany said. She wiped a tear from her face as she pulled away. Then she forced a laugh as she looked at the wet spot on her hand. "Sorry about making things awkward."

Esther laughed. To her surprise, it wasn't forced at all.

"No worries," she said. "I don't know if I've ever made a friend so fast in my life."

They smiled at each other, then went their separate ways.

Disaster wasn't a strong enough word to describe the state of the pastor's office. It smelled like feet and lotion. A bookshelf full of old, dull-looking books covered an entire wall. The shelves sagged as if they might collapse at any moment under the weight of outdated theology. The surface of the desk was scattered with papers and mountains of receipts. Next to a nameplate that read *REVEREND TEDDY ROSS* was a bowl of peppermint candies that looked like it was on the verge of falling off one corner of the desk.

"Please come in and sit," the pastor said, without standing. "Would you like a candy?"

Esther took a seat in one of the two chairs in front of the desk. She leaned close to the bowl to inspect the red and white striped treats. The candies were peppermint puffs, and they were not individually wrapped. They also looked old, like they had been on the desk for a long time.

"No. Thank you."

The pastor reached for one of the peppermint puffs. He had to really dig with his fingers for the one he wanted, because they were all stuck together. He pried his peppermint from the rest as if he was pulling a diamond from a cave wall, and then threw it in his mouth.

"Don't mind if I do," he said to himself.

Esther could hear the mint knocking against his teeth and mixing with his saliva as he sucked on it.

"You like my little slice of Heaven?" he asked, spinning slightly in his chair to gesture at the office. He was bald with a white beard and very large. Probably at least three hundred pounds. He didn't necessarily look obese—rather, he looked like a football lineman that had let himself go. He was also very sweaty. Esther wondered if he might be sick.

She swiveled her head in an exaggerated manner, to take in the sights of the office again. *More like a little slice of Hell.*

"It's lovely," she lied.

The most attention-seeking object in the office, other than the pastor, was hung on the wall directly behind the man's head. It was a framed portrait of former President Donald Trump. The president was sitting at his desk in the Oval Office, signing something. Jesus stood behind him, one nail-pierced hand resting upon Trump's shoulder. A look of utmost satisfaction adorned the savior's face.

He wants me to comment on it.

"I see you're admiring my art," the pastor said without looking at it.

"It's... something else," Esther said. "Personally, I—"

"The man was done dirty," the pastor continued. It was like he had interrupted her on purpose. He used his thumb to point behind him. "That man was the only hope for our country."

"Are you referring to Trump? Or Jesus?"

Pastor Teddy crossed his arms over his chest. He used his thumb and pointer finger to tug at his white beard as if he was thinking deeply about her question.

"Touché," he said with a shake of his head. "I take it you voted for Biden in the last election."

Wow, this got inappropriate real quick.

"Yes," she answered. "What gave me away?"

"Your skin color for one." He blurted out without an ounce of trepidation. "The Democrats have most of the non-white population fooled into thinking they have their best interests in mind. You are a Democrat, are you not?"

"Actually, I consider myself more of—"

"And another reason is because of how young you are." The man wouldn't even let her answer the questions that *he* asked her.

"I'm forty years old," she objected.

"Last but not least," he continued, "that rainbow pin you're wearing. It's a sure sign that you've gone woke. Woke people voted for Biden. It's just a fact."

Esther touched the pin on her lapel. She felt like a kid sitting in Sunday-school class again. Her front teeth wanted to gnaw at the knuckles on her right hand. It had been years since she had given in to that old habit.

"Are you alright?" Pastor Teddy asked.

Esther placed her hands in her lap and crossed her legs. She looked the man directly in his blue eyes. They were the same color as her father's eyes.

"I'm fine," she said. "But let's get on with it. You've seen my resume. You also see my tattoos and rainbow pin. Why on earth would you even consider hiring me?"

"Well. I suppose it's because I'm looking to bring in... a certain person."

Esther sat back in her chair. "A certain person?"

"Excuse me," the pastor said. "I meant to say a certain *type* of person."

"What type of person are we talking about?"

Pastor Teddy's eyes narrowed like he was trying to figure her out. "Maybe someone you know."

"Who do I know?" Esther inquired. She leaned forward in her chair, her hands gripping the armrests tightly. "You've never hired a female pastor before. I checked when I saw that you were hiring. Why interview *me*? I'll probably just *disappear*."

Pastor Teddy scratched his chest. "Disappear? Whatever do you mean?"

"I mean just what I said. I've noticed that women tend to leave this church after a while."

"It's not a prison!" the pastor exclaimed. "People are free to come and go as they choose."

"But why are these women leaving?"

"They went *woke*." Pastor Teddy spat out the word as if it was a curse. "They stopped believing the Bible. I'm sure there's a number of reasons."

"They stopped believing *your* interpretation of the Bible?"

"There is only one interpretation."

Esther wanted to argue, but let it go. "How did you respond when these women went *woke*? It obviously upset you. Did you do anything to them?"

"What do you mean, 'do anything'?"

"Like, maybe you confronted them. Called them out?"

"I didn't do anything. They all just went to different churches."

"Did they?" Esther asked. "Because I couldn't find any record of—"

"What are you? Some kind of journalist for some progressive magazine?"

Pastor Teddy stood. Esther was forced to look up to maintain eye contact. She decided to stand as well. The hair on her arms did the same. She was getting bad vibes. It was time to leave.

"I think I'll show myself out." She made a move toward the exit. "This interview was a bad idea."

To Esther's surprise, the giant man began to cry. Tears rolled down his cheeks and disappeared into his beard.

"Please wait," he said. There was something new in his voice. A vulnerability she hadn't thought him capable of. "I want to hire you because this place needs to change. I need to change. I know it. I just have a hard time admitting it."

Esther's eyebrows raised.

The pastor motioned at her seat. "Please, sit back down for just a moment."

Reluctantly, she sat.

"When I became the pastor of this church many years ago, I truly hoped to help people." His head hung low. It was like he was no longer willing to make eye contact. "I wanted to be the hands and feet of... of... that man." He pointed at the picture hung on the wall behind him. "Somewhere along the way, I lost my way." He picked up a handful of receipts from his desk and then slapped them back down. "I became more of a businessman. And then, my daughter..."

Esther leaned in. His vulnerability was working. She felt a strong desire to comfort him. At the mention of his daughter, his subtle crying had turned into more of a sob.

"She... she..." He was having a hard time getting the words out. "She came out of the closet a while ago. She left the church, and now she lives in Montgomery with her girlfriend."

Esther's eyes widened at the confession. She had not expected this turn.

Pastor Teddy took a deep breath. The worst of his crying seemed to be over. He was trying to get ahold of himself.

"I know I handled the whole thing very poorly. I haven't talked to her in over a year. She won't return my texts. She won't come home for the holidays. My wife died of cancer a while back, and my daughter is all I have. I miss her so much."

Esther's heart hurt, as if she was part of this man's family. Yes, it hurt for Pastor Teddy, but it also hurt for the poor daughter. The entire situation was lamentable and she longed for a day when scenarios like this were a thing of the distant past.

"I'm hoping that having a person like you on staff will help me change. It will help this church take a massive step in the right direction."

And you want me to facilitate a reconciliation with your daughter, instead of doing the work all by yourself, she thought.

"I'm aware of this church's reputation," Pastor Teddy said. "I've heard the rumors of us making women 'disappear.' Look, I'm abrasive, and I believe that men should be the ones in charge. At least, I used to believe that. But I'm changing. If you want the job, it's yours. I promise to shut up and listen to what you have to say. What do you think?"

Esther didn't quite know how to respond. Yes, she had been caught off guard by the pastor's sudden change in demeanor, but even more, she had been shaken by the fact that some part of her actually wanted the job.

She remembered the reason she was here. Dalton was still sitting out in the parking lot, waiting for her to return and spill the beans on how these people were up to something truly evil. He was probably losing his mind right about now, imagining her being chased by demons or drowned in the baptismal font. Also, she hadn't forgotten that she already had a job that she loved. But still, she couldn't help but imagine herself as a pastor. Not one that got up on stage above everyone else and paraded around in the limelight, spouting hate disguised as love. No—one that was much more like a good shepherd. One who would feed the hungry. Comfort the broken-hearted. One who truly tried to follow in Christ's footsteps.

"Well?" Pastor Teddy asked again.

Is that hope in his voice?

"Maybe," she answered.

The pastor slapped his desk. Papers flew into the air.

"Hot dog!" he exclaimed. "That's better than a no."

Esther actually chuckled.

"When can you start?"

Her head bowed a bit. She looked down at her feet. The spiritual conviction that so often accompanied old-time religion came on fast. It was as if the Holy Spirit had whispered into her ear that she was unforgivably sinful for deceiving a reverend.

She looked up. Arguably, Pastor Teddy wasn't a good person. Still, it did seem he was interested in changing. And now she was in his church, lying to him about possibly accepting a job, all while trying to figure out if Dalton's dreams about Pastor Teddy being a murderer of women, or a rapist, or whatever, were true.

"I need a while to think about it."

I need a while to decide if you're genuine, she thought.

"That's no problem at all," the pastor said. "We'll have an ordination service. Let's say... three months from now? I'll have Brittany text you the details."

He was acting like himself again. He pried another peppermint puff from the bowl on his desk and threw it into his mouth.

"Pray about it. I want you to be sure of this decision. If you show up to the ordination—and I sure hope you do—the job is yours, and we can start actually doing some good around here."

DALTON'S DREAM
ONE YEAR BEFORE ORDINATION

The concept of omnipresence is too complicated for the human mind, and yet every Christian kid believes they understand it completely. God's ways are not our ways, but we have almost infinite means of explaining his ways to our small-minded selves. Jesus is God, and therefore he is everywhere. The way Dalton's childhood brain had accepted this notion was to picture Christ in multiples. He imagined Jesus as the first of the X-Men, and one of his many superpowers was creating unlimited copies of himself so that he could be anywhere and everywhere at once.

Thirteen-year-old Dalton was currently staring at seven of them. Seven saviors. All with long brown hair and beards. All of them wearing matching off-white tunics. Seven pairs of brown sandals adorned the feet of the ones that would walk the earth and leave God-shaped footprints behind.

"Come to me," the Jesuses chimed in perfect unison.

Dalton took in his surroundings. There *were* no surroundings. There was nothing. He was in a pitch-black void.

Now the earth was formless and void, and darkness was over the surface of the deep.

Dalton turned his attention back to the Jesuses.

"Which one of you shall I go to?" he asked. His frail voice bounced off the dark walls of pre-creation.

"Come to me," the seven Jesuses said as one. They communicated like robots with preprogrammed responses.

Is it possible to choose incorrectly? Dalton wondered.

They were each God. Therefore, they were each good. But if that were true, why did Dalton feel he could make a wrong decision? The saviors each took a step forward. The black floor where their feet landed rippled like water when a stone is thrown in. They stretched their hands toward Dalton. He could see nail marks in their palms.

"Come to me."

Dalton took a step back. Jesus was his friend and yet here, wherever he was, whenever he was, he was afraid.

"Do not be afraid." They each took a second step forward. "Give me your hand."

"Which one of you is the real Jesus?" Dalton shouted.

"I am," they all said.

The atmosphere of the nothing-place shook with the statement. He had been afraid before in his short life. What he experienced now was more than simple fear. It was primal. Something important was happening. He had a choice to make. A choice that, for some reason, he knew could have an impact on the future. If he picked the wrong Jesus, he would be damning not only himself, but all those who would search for salvation. At this point in creation, everyone that would ever be was counting on him.

"Who is real?" Dalton shouted at the group. "Show me proof!"

They moved, approaching him speedily and then surrounding him. Their nail-pierced hands reached for him. Their fingertips stopped mere inches away from his face.

"Choose this day whom you will serve. Choose. Choose. Choose. Choose."

Dalton had no clue which Jesus to choose. Not ready to make a decision, he looked away. He focused on the floor beneath him, wanting to scream, "Go away!"

Instead, he screamed for help. He had begun to sink. Slowly, the nonexistent floor began to swallow him like a black hole.

He looked up.

"Jesus. I need you! Save me!"

His lower half was no longer visible. He couldn't feel his legs. It was as if they had never existed in the first place.

What are *legs?*

The Jesuses continued to reach for him.

"Choose. Choose. Choose. Choose."

Dalton sank further into the abyss. His chest and shoulders vanished outside time and space. He was up to his neck in annihilation. He now existed only as a head and two unattached arms reaching out of a tar pit at the beginning of time.

"Choose. Choose. Choose. Choose."

Dalton picked a Jesus randomly, and reached for him. The other Jesuses disappeared. Dalton's personal savior grabbed him and pulled him upwards. His shoulders and chest were created anew as he emerged from the blackness.

Jesus looked deep into Dalton's eyes. Dalton stared back at him, refusing to look away. The story in the Bible when Peter briefly walked on water slid into his mind. Dalton, like Peter, had sunk only when he had taken his eyes off Jesus and focused on his surroundings. He had learned his lesson. He would turn his eyes upon Jesus and he would never look away again.

"Thank you!" Dalton exclaimed.

Jesus said nothing.

"Jesus?" Dalton asked, "are you going to pull me the rest of the way out?"

Jesus leaned in close to Dalton's ear. Dalton could feel the breath of creation against the side of his face. It smelled like grapes.

"You of little faith," a still, small voice whispered into his ear. "Why did you doubt?"

Jesus put a hand on top of Dalton's head. A pressure that could not be resisted pushed Dalton down. His chest and shoulders were once again obliterated. His neck, chin, and nose were all erased from existence. The last thing he saw was the face of his savior turned destructor. It wasn't Jesus' face at all. It was the face of a demon. Her eyes glowed a dull red. Scraggly hair poked out of a dirty hood that covered the monstrosity's head and framed her face. Two deer-like antlers looked as if they had ripped through the hood and shot toward the sky. She grinned with a mouth full of blackened teeth.

"Hello, Dalton," the witch growled in her gravelly yet playful voice. "I'm back. Come and find me."

You! Dalton thought, before his mind was submerged and he ceased to be.

***

"Dalton!" Esther screamed. She shook him even harder this time. He still didn't wake up. His body continued to convulse in the bed. The bed frame shook and the headboard kept slamming against the bedroom wall.

"Dalton!" she screamed for what seemed the hundredth time. She swung her left leg over his body and straddled him. She could see his pupils through the tiny open slits of his eyelids. They were darting around as if he were searching for something to save his life.

"Jesus. I need you. Save me!" Dalton screamed in his sleep.

Esther grabbed the sides of his face and used the inside part of her elbows and knees to try and stabilize his body. It felt as if she were trying to ride a rodeo bull.

I need to call 911, she decided.

Dalton's eyes popped wide open.

"You!" he shrieked.

His hands rocketed up and wrapped around Esther's throat. Immediately, she couldn't breathe. She grabbed his wrist and tried pulling his hands away, but they wouldn't budge.

"Dal... ton." she rasped.

The name barely escaped her lips. He was looking right at her, but it was also like he was looking past her. His expression scared her—he looked like he was deciding if he should kill her.

His grip tightened. He had made up his mind.

"Dal..."

She couldn't talk. Her chest burned as if she had swallowed acid. Her vision started to blur.

This is happening... too fast, she thought. *I should have... had more time to try... and escape.*

She beat weakly at Dalton's chest and arms. Nothing she tried made him stop. She couldn't make him see her. She knew he was still dreaming. This wasn't the first of his nightmares she had endured. This *was* the first that had become physical, though, and if she didn't think of something to wake him up, it would also be the last.

Using what little strength she had left, she buried her right knee in his groin. She could feel his scrotum flatten. The pressure around her neck loosened. She fell on her back and then rolled off the bed onto the carpeted floor. She wanted to lie there. She needed time to recover, but she also wasn't certain what headspace Dalton was in. She jumped to her feet and got into a defensive position with her arms raised in front of her.

"Esther?" Dalton said. His body was scrunched up in the fetal position in the middle of the mattress. He was holding his groin area.

"Dalton? Are you back?"

He sat up and looked at Esther. His eyes went wide. His mouth opened and sucked in air. She could see the realization of what he had done dawning on him.

"Oh my God!" he shouted. He leapt out of bed and moved toward her. "Did I— Are you okay? I'm so sorry, Esther!"

Esther backed up. Her hands remained raised in front of her.

"Stay back!"

Dalton froze.

"Esther," he said. "There's no excuse. I don't know what to say."

She lowered her hands a bit.

"I'll go sleep on the couch," Dalton said. "Or I can leave if you need me to."

"No," Esther said. Even that small word hurt, scraping out of her as if it had used fingernails to crawl past her throat. "Don't leave."

She dropped her hands and cleared her throat. Her voice sounded like that of a lifelong chain-smoker. Esther had never touched a cigarette. "We have stuff to talk about."

"Okay," Dalton said. He put his hands up with his palms facing her, most likely trying to make himself look less intimidating. It was the correct thing for him to do in the moment, for his own protection. If he had made any move Esther didn't approve of, she would have kicked him in his groin so hard that the vasectomy he had had a few years ago wouldn't be the only thing keeping him from having kids.

"Let's go downstairs to talk," she coughed out. "I suddenly don't feel like being in this bedroom anymore."

She turned and walked out of the room. Dalton followed her at a safe, non-threatening distance.

"So, I had another bad dream," he said as they entered the living room.

Esther turned and gave him a death stare.

"No shit."

IT'S ORDINATION DAY!

The night was black. The moon was full and large in the sky. Dalton pulled the car into the same space in the parking lot as he had three months ago. Her undercover interview with Pastor Teddy seemed a lifetime ago. She looked at the church and sighed.

"Are you ready?" Dalton asked.

"I'm ready for this to be over," she answered. "I'm going in there to tell Pastor Teddy that I prayed about it, and the Lord has led me in a different direction. For your sake, I'll play along for a few minutes before I do that. I don't think this pastor is a great leader or anything. But I also don't think he's doing what you think he is. The women all probably bounced because he's a grade-A misogynist."

"But we couldn't get in contact with a single one of them!" Dalton yelled at an unnecessary volume.

Esther shushed him. "I know. That's why I'll play along for just a bit longer. They probably just got off social media. So, if I don't see something suspicious fairly soon once I'm in there, I'm out."

Dalton was about to protest. He lifted a finger to make a point but Esther lifted her phone up and blocked him out of her vision. She used the camera on her phone to check her appearance. She was wearing the same outfit she had worn the day of her fake interview, but this time she had thrown a black hoodie over it.

"They aren't going to be happy about your hoodie," Dalton told her.

"I don't care." She put her phone in the front pocket of her hoodie, then retrieved a black hair tie from the same pocket. She used it to secure as much of her thick hair into a tight ponytail as would cooperate.

"It's freaking cold in there," she said. "And this isn't a real ordination, anyway."

"I don't think it's real either," he agreed.

"No, Dalton," she snapped. "What I mean is I'm not taking this job."

"Obviously."

"No. You're not understanding me. The more I think about it, the more I think we've been acting..."

She paused. Her eyes met Dalton's.

"Crazy," he muttered, finishing her sentence for her. He shook his head. "You think I'm crazy."

Her heart thumped heavy in her chest. She reached for Dalton and placed her hands on his cheeks.

"No. I don't think you're crazy."

Dalton placed his hands on top of hers.

"I truly don't." She forced him to look at her. "But babe, trauma stays in our bodies for a long time. The same is true of religious trauma. You haven't been yourself for a while now. Even before the dreams. You're not crazy, but I do think it's time for you to go back to therapy."

Dalton pulled away. He grabbed the steering wheel with both hands and squeezed it hard. It looked as if he were about to attempt to rip it off the steering column. A low growl that had the potential to turn into a primal scream of rage rumbled in his throat. Before the growl could evolve, Dalton seemed to return to himself. The noise stopped and his hands relaxed on the wheel.

"You're right," he said. He took a deep breath. "I've known that since the night I strangled you. But I had more dreams. The dreams where Uncle Marvin told me about the women of this church. And the witch is back. It's my job to..."

Esther put her hand on his chest. He stopped talking.

"The witch isn't back, Dalton. Don't forget. You beat her."

"But she's returned once already," he said. He now sounded more defeated than manic. "James had to..."

"What would your therapist say?" Esther interjected.

Dalton swallowed hard and leaned back in his seat with his head pressed firmly against the headrest.

"I know. I know." He rubbed at his temples. "If she comes back, it's because my mind is bringing her back. She only has power over me if I give it to her."

Esther leaned over and kissed him on his forehead.

"That's right," she said. "Don't let her get to you."

"I'm sorry." Dalton closed his eyes. "I'm sorry for this past year. For what I've put you through. For how I've been acting. It's all insane. I see that now."

He sat upright.

"Let's just go."

He cranked the car.

"No," Esther said. "Turn the engine off."

Without waiting, she reached over and took the key out of the ignition.

"I'm gonna finish what *we* started."

She handed the keys back to Dalton. "Just promise me you'll stay here until I get back. Then we can go visit your family and maybe talk to James about getting you on some meds."

"Okay," Dalton said. "Sounds like a plan to me."

***

Esther entered the church through the same door she had used on her first visit. The foyer was still cold. The hoodie was a good idea.

"Hello!" she called out. Her voice echoed. The place reminded her of a cave. The banners hanging from the ceiling made her think of stalactites. She realized she was actually pleased that no one answered her call.

"This place is creepy at night," she said to herself. She wasn't sure quite what made the empty foyer so off-putting. Nothing appeared threatening. On the contrary, everything seemed super inviting. Every couch begged to be sat in. Every bit of signage featured people with smiling faces, as if to make sure no one felt unwelcome. Still, *she* felt unwelcome. The fake-smiling fake people were lying to her.

She had texted Brittany to say that she would arrive in the foyer promptly at 9 PM on Saturday, October 14th, the date and time Brittany had told her to arrive. The time seemed late for an ordination, but then again, Esther had never been ordained before. She wasn't really sure what the ceremony would entail.

She checked the time on her phone. It was ten past eight. Her premature arrival time was part of Dalton's plan. If possible, she was to poke around a bit before the ceremony began.

She texted Brittany.

I'm at the church early. Are you here yet? Would like to talk to you before the ordination.

Three dots, and then a response came through.

What?

***

Dalton sat in the car. The engine was off but the key was in the ignition so he could listen to music. His window was down and the night air was perfect with just a bit of coolness in it. Sitting in the parking lot of this church, on this particular property, he should have been reeling with anxiety. Instead, he was a touch nostalgic. His time in church as a young person hadn't been all bad. There were good memories. And everything had worked out for the good. Especially Esther. He would never have ended up with a woman like her if his past hadn't chased him into her arms. She was good for him. He loved her. Her last words before she had exited the car had calmed him. He was suddenly ready to put his year-long lapse into evangelical madness behind him. Of course he was reading too much into this. He was making something out of nothing, like a conservative Christian watching a Super Bowl halftime show. Satanic panic was not a shade that looked good on him.

The car's Bluetooth was connected to his phone, and his music app kept shuffling songs. Inspired by his nostalgic mood, he had selected a Christian rock playlist he had created and named *Tooth & Nail*. The song currently playing was by a band called Poor Old Lu. Dalton tapped his foot on the brake pedal. He had forgotten how much he loved this band. He cranked up the volume.

***

The bottoms of Esther's feet tingled like needles were poking into them as she speed walked down the long corridor. She had taken off her high heels after just a few steps. The sound they made against the polished concrete floor was too loud, and she was afraid someone other than Brittany might hear her. Holding her shoes, she moved past a metal door on her left with a plaque above it that read, *Nursing Mothers' Room*. To her right was the first of the doors labeled *Sanctuary*. She looked at her phone. Eight-twelve. She needed to pick up the pace if she wanted to get a look at the pastor's office without him in it.

Maybe there's a hidden safe behind that horrendous picture of Jesus and Trump, containing evidence of his crimes?

She knew the thought was ridiculous. She knew she wasn't currently living out an episode of *Scooby-Doo*. If she had the chance, though, she would definitely check behind the picture. She picked up her pace, her bare feet slapping against the floor. After passing many more doors, the end of the hallway came into view. The track-mounted wooden door with the cross carved into it was shut. She slowed to a jog as she approached it. She was breathing heavily.

I need to go back to the gym, she thought.

The door was locked.

"Dammit!" she exclaimed, louder than she should have. She yanked at the door, knowing full well it was a useless gesture.

Where is Brittany? she thought. *Maybe she has a key.*

She pulled out her phone. She had a new text from Brittany.

Ordination? I'll meet you in the sanctuary. Stay there.

Esther answered *OK*, then put her phone away.

"What am I doing here?" she asked herself. She turned and slammed her back against the door. Her body slid down its surface until her butt hit the floor. She sat in silence for a moment. The silence was broken by her own laughter.

"We deserve each other, Dalton."

She put her high heels back on and stood. It was time to leave this place and, unlike Lot's wife in the Bible, never look back. She would just stop by the sanctuary real quick and tell Brittany, and Brittany could notify the pastor on Esther's behalf.

***

Dalton's phone buzzed. As he read the text message, relief washed over him.

Found nothing unusual. On my way out. Just wanna talk to Brittany first.

The words carried away his worries like an ocean wave pulling litter from a beach. In a few moments, he and Esther would put this church and his relapse into madness in the rear-view mirror.

A bright, brief flash of silver light filled the transparent dome on top of the daycare building.

"What the hell?"

He opened his door and sprang out of the car to get a better look.

"What was that?"

The light reappeared. This time it appeared almost golden. It flashed on and off with no discernible pattern.

Maybe an alarm is going off in the daycare? he thought.

In between flashes, he could make out the silhouette of the dome in the dark. He squinted, finding he couldn't look away. A memory creeped into his consciousness. He remembered a boy strapped into an electric chair. He could still see the electricity coursing through the boy's body. Sparks had flown as the kid convulsed. Smoke rose from his cooking skin, which blackened and popped like meat left on a grill for too long. The smell of smoldering flesh and hair once again assaulted Dalton's nostrils.

I pollute the pond, Dalton.

Shame and guilt reached from the past and grabbed ahold of him. It forced him to briefly look away. Of course that kid hadn't actually died in the electric chair. The entire scene had been part of a hallucination that his subconscious mind had conjured to deal with his father's abusive tendencies when Dalton was thirteen. He had lost contact with the boy in the years after. Sadly, the last he had heard of his old childhood friend was that he had become a junkie and died of a drug overdose.

What was that guy's name?

The light in the dome continued to flash. He lifted his hands to shield his eyes.

The sound of a car door slamming startled him. He turned quickly to his car. The driver's-side door was shut.

"Esther?"

A hand poked out of the driver's-side window. It beckoned him to get in.

I don't care who drives, he thought. *Let's get out of here.*

"Coming," he said.

He took one last look at the strange, flickering lights and then headed for the passenger side of the car. He opened the door, flung himself into the seat, and slammed the door shut.

"So," he said while buckling his seatbelt, "you apologized to this Brittany girl and told her you don't want the job?"

Esther didn't answer. She also didn't move. Her hands gripped the steering wheel firmly at the ten and two positions. She was facing forward and her hair was down. Dalton couldn't even see her face.

"Um, Esther? Are you okay? Did something happen?"

Her shoulders and arms began to shake. It looked like the beginning of a seizure. He reached for her.

"What's wrong?" he said with urgency. "What happened in there?"

Memories of shadowy demons with glowing lava-like blood oozing underneath cracked, blackened skin assaulted him. A witch riding a headless deer trotted through his imagination. The night spent in his father's haunted church, the church that used to stand on this very property, replayed in his mind.

As Esther turned, the bones in her neck cracked loudly. The area around her face was surrounded by a mane of messy, black hair.

Her face... wasn't *her* face. In its place was the countenance of a demon. But not just any demon.

"Your friend's name was Kirk," the witch snarled. Her eyes glowed red and her teeth were black. As she leaned toward Dalton, antlers sprouted out of her head. The hair that had moments ago been much like Esther's, fell down as if it were withering and dying. It straightened into greasy strands of grayish black.

Dalton recoiled. The back of his head slammed into the door frame. He opened the door and struggled to exit the vehicle, but his seatbelt held him in place.

The witch cackled. "Kirk's in Hell, Dalton! I've seen him. And it's all your fault!"

Dalton's hands fumbled to unbuckle his seatbelt. He couldn't find the release button.

"It's all your fault! It's all your fault!"

The seatbelt unfastened with a loud click. The witch's bony hands reached toward Dalton, but he jerked away from her and tumbled out of the vehicle. His elbows exploded with pain like they were grenades triggered upon impact with the ground. His back slammed into and then scraped against the asphalt of the parking lot. His right ankle was caught under the hinge of the car door.

The witch reached for his foot. Dalton yanked it away and his shoe came off. The witch grabbed the shoe and hugged it as if it were a childhood toy that she missed dearly.

Dalton got to his feet and ran toward the church.

I have to find Esther! It was the only thought that kept him moving.

From behind him, he could hear the witch's continued laughter and taunts. "Like your pedo-daddy said, Dalton. Generational curses! I'm yours. I'm all yours!"

Dalton had almost reached the door of the church, but he couldn't help turning to take a last look at his nemesis. He wasn't entirely sure if she was really there. But when he looked, he saw her on her knees in the passenger seat of his vehicle, where he had been only moments before. She pulled her tattered cloak up to her shoulders, exposing herself. Dalton was surprised at how slender and fit her body was. It was attractive, with one exception. Her left breast was wrinkled and blackened. It looked like a rotten vegetable. It sagged to a much lower position than her right breast, which appeared round and perky. The witch grabbed both of them and lifted them toward her mouth. Her tongue shot out and slithered across the scab-like nipple of her rotten tit. Yellow pus oozed out like spoiled milk and dripped down her body. At the same time, bright white milk squirted out of the nipple of her right breast and arched through the air toward him, as if it had been shot from a water pistol. Dalton turned and ran to the door he had seen Esther enter earlier.

"No one knows the day nor the hour!" the witch screamed from behind him. "But I always return!"

***

Despite having passed through the sanctuary doors, Esther still couldn't see the actual sanctuary. The passage reminded her of the kind that a basketball team would run out of to make their grand entrance onto the court. After about thirty feet the walkway ended and the sanctuary finally came into view. It was massive. She imagined herself a spelunker that had just discovered a new cavern. The explanation she had been given for why the church was kept so cold now made sense. Controlling the temperature of a room this humongous must be quite a task. There were rows and rows of chairs. How many? She couldn't even formulate a guess. The chairs were lined up perfectly into different squared sections. She did a quick spin around and noticed even more chairs behind her. A balcony stretched almost all the way up to the very high roof. The chairs in the balcony looked like the seats in a movie theater. The roof was littered with all kinds of impressive-looking lighting. Many of the lamps appeared to be connected to narrow walkways hooked to the ceiling that looked to Esther like bridges high up in the sky. Her vision spun just looking up at them.

A stage acted as the focal point of the place. It was currently blocked from view by a massive, dark blue curtain. Esther walked toward it. The farther she moved into the auditorium, the more it dawned on her that she was but a speck in the universe.

Who am I that you should be mindful of me?

It was as if she was responding to an altar call that she hadn't even heard.

"I'm sorry, God," she said as she walked along a row of chairs. She ran her hand across the top of each chair as she passed. "I'm not even sure what for. But I know that I'm sorry. I have doubts and questions. But there is something inside me that won't let go of you. And I don't think you've ever let go of me."

She paused and looked up. She was still a good fifty feet from the foot of the stage.

"Brittany?" she whisper-shouted.

There was no response. Esther looked around her. The air was cold against her eyeballs. She waited for at least ten minutes for her friend to show up, but she never did.

"I can't wait any longer."

She decided to leave and just text Brittany her decision, but before she took a single step, a crash of thunder reverberated throughout the auditorium. Her body tensed. The sound had been that of a horn or some kind of trumpet. But it was unlike any trumpet she had ever heard. For a moment, she imagined it was a divine trumpet heralding the return of Christ.

There's no time to change your mind. The time has come, and you've been left behind.

She half expected to see the dead in Christ begin to rise. Dalton had told her that his family had a small cemetery on this property that was bulldozed to make this mega-church. She imagined seeing Dalton's grandparents' souls floating up into the rafters and then exiting through the roof. She was looking up when she heard a blood curdling scream.

"What the…"

The scream had come from behind the closed curtain.

Is someone on the stage? Esther wondered. *Is Brittany hurt?*

She kicked off her heels, which flew in different directions, and ran to the foot of the stage. She jumped up with all her might, and her elbows landed on the edge of the wooden stage. It was high, and she had barely been able to jump high enough to get her elbows in place. Her triceps burned as she pulled herself up. She almost slipped off, the fabric of her hoodie slick against the polished wood. Her belly and knees scraped against the wooden edge as she rolled onto the stage. Now all that stood before her and whoever had been hurt was the thick fabric of the stage curtains.

"The scripture is clear!" a booming male voice shouted. "A woman cannot preach. Paul's first letter to Timothy teaches that a woman must remain quiet."

Esther rose to her feet and grabbed the fabric curtain. Her fingertips danced across it, looking for an opening. When she failed to find one, she dropped back onto her stomach and lifted the heavy curtain just enough to peek underneath it.

What she saw was a scene straight out of a horror movie. A young blonde girl was stripped naked and strapped onto a makeshift altar. The girl kicked wildly and jerked against the bonds holding her down. The altar appeared to be nothing more than an overturned podium, a big wooden pulpit from which a preacher would deliver his sermon. It appeared blackened in a few places, possibly burn marks.

"Help me!" the girl screamed. "Please, don't do this. I won't be a pastor. I changed my mind!"

A figure in a dark brown cloak stood over her. A hood pulled over the head hid their face in shadow. The figure towered over the woman like a Philistine giant. A black shirt with a preacher's collar was visible beneath the hood, just under the unseen face. Judging by the body type, Esther had a good idea who was under the cloak. It had to be Pastor Teddy. He was holding a large knife over his head with both hands.

Dalton's dreams were right!

"Female pastors don't break glass ceilings," he said. He spoke the words without anger or irritation; it was more like he was simply teaching a lesson or making a point in a sermon. "They break God's commands. You have spoken of your desire to be a worship pastor on multiple occasions. You have left this leadership no choice."

"Amen," a collection of voices said.

Esther looked beyond the pastor. She had been so entranced by Pastor Teddy with a knife raised above an unclothed woman that she had failed to notice the other figures standing around the altar. They all stood eerily still and wore identical brown cloaks. Many of them hugged large Bibles to their chests. One lifted a trumpet, which looked like it had been carved from an animal's horn, to their lips and blew. Pastor Teddy's knife rocketed downward. The girl turned her head and screamed. Her eyes found Esther's.

Brittany!

For the briefest of moments, she saw a flash of hope in Brittany's eyes. The hope vanished at the same time the knife plunged into her chest. Blood spurted out and rolled down her peach-colored flesh in messy red lines. Pastor Teddy let go of the knife, leaving it buried in her.

"Es... ther... Find... me," Brittany whispered hoarsely with her dying breath. She reached toward Esther, but then her arm fell and hit the stage with a thud as the life left her body.

The dark areas beneath the hoods of the cloaked figures turned to Brittany's dead hand, then to where it was pointing—to Esther's face spying on them from under the stage curtain.

"Well, well, well," Pastor Teddy said. He reached over and jerked the knife from Brittany's chest. Her body rose a bit, as if holding onto the knife, then collapsed back onto the pulpit as it slid out. Droplets of blood dripped from the blade as Pastor Teddy pointed its tip at Esther. "You showed up."

He took a step toward her. His dark associates did the same. Their footfalls shook the wood floor against which Esther's body was pressed.

"Happy ordination day," Pastor Teddy growled.

Esther dropped the curtain, rolled off the stage, and landed on the floor on all fours like a cat. Pain travelled up and then back down all her limbs. She had no time to dwell on it. She stood and ran away, as if responding to a reverse altar call.

The neon green exit signs above the doorways that led out of the sanctuary represented salvation, but they were so very far away. Esther turned to look behind her. Pastor Teddy held the curtain up while his followers leaped off the stage and gave chase.

Fuck. They're fast!

She turned away and focused on fleeing. She had planned to take a direct route straight up the center aisle, but somehow one of the figures was now standing ten feet in front of her, blocking her way.

Esther darted into a row of chairs to her right. The figure followed. At the other end of the row, a second hooded person blocked her way. It was as if she were in a real-life game of *Pac-Man*. The two figures began to close in on either side of her. She climbed onto the seat of a chair and hurtled over its back to land on the seat of the chair in the row directly behind. Her foot sank into the seat cushion as she landed, but she continued to leap from chair to chair like a hurdler until she had cleared the seating area. She sprinted along the open aisle toward the exit, the two pursuers at her heels. She saw another moving in from a side aisle. They were like predators working as a team to make a kill.

As they closed in, Esther realized she wouldn't be able to outrun them, so she swerved at the last second and dove under a chair. She army-crawled under chairs as fast as she could manage. Her knees and elbows throbbed as they slammed frantically against the floor. She could hear the movements of the hooded figures. It sounded like they were standing on the chairs and leaping over them from row to row, as she had earlier.

She couldn't crawl fast enough—they would be on top of her at any moment. She would have to stand and run.

As soon as she stood, she was tackled. Her back struck the floor between the rows of chairs with a thud. Her attacker shoved their left knee into her gut and their right knee rested on the seat of a chair. Hands pressed hard against her throat. Esther tried to lift her head, and managed a slight movement, but the back of her neck remained pressed against the floor. She scratched and clawed at her attacker's arms and face. The hood came away. Her attacker was a guy with a bushy mustache.

No matter how hard she hit him, he wouldn't budge. She pulled out a clump of his hair. He didn't flinch. His eyes grew large, and sweat dripped from his forehead.

Esther's vision blurred. She tried kicking him in the balls. It didn't work. Her blows were becoming weaker and weaker. She was fading fast. The man's face was blurry now. It looked as though he had multiple mustaches. Esther's throat burned. She reached out in desperation. As her hand fumbled under one of the seats, her fingers touched something that felt familiar. She grabbed it and, with all the strength she had left, swung it up at the man's head.

He collapsed on top of her.

Esther crawled out from under him, her breathing heavy. She rose to her feet and looked down at him.

"Holy Shit!" She exclaimed.

She had to grab onto the back of a chair to steady herself as dizziness and shock overwhelmed her.

The man appeared dead. One of her high-heeled shoes was stuck deep in his temple. He groaned.

Esther didn't waste a second. She slipped her foot into the shoe still sticking out of the man's head, as if she was Cinderella trying on a glass slipper. She pressed down, hard. With a satisfying squishing sound, the heel pressed in even farther. She imagined it puncturing the man's brain. She rotated her ankle a few times for good measure.

Blessed are the feet.

When someone grabbed her from behind, she lifted her foot up and her high-heeled shoe withdrew from the dead man's temple. Blood spouted out of the tiny hole like a miniature geyser. She stomped her bloody heel into the shoe of the person holding her from behind.

They howled in pain. She hoped the heel had gone straight through their foot, like a crucifixion nail. Their grip loosened, but didn't release her. She went limp, like she had been taught to do in a self-defense class she had taken years ago.

It worked. She dropped to the ground, and when she looked up, her attacker was holding her empty hoodie. She slammed her elbow into the high-heeled shoe still stuck in the person's foot. He screamed and bent over in pain. She pulled the heel out of their foot and shoved it into their throat, right next to an Adam's apple. She moved out of the way by rolling onto a chair as the man fell face first to land on top of the other body.

"Get her!" a booming voice commanded. Esther was certain the voice belonged to Pastor Teddy directing his minion.

She ran faster than she had ever run before. A single hooded figure still pursued her, and she had a good enough lead that she just might make it to safety. As she entered the walkway that led out of the sanctuary, hope bloomed in her heart. She was going to make it. She chanced a look back at her pursuer. They were too far back. She would be out of the sanctuary, through the foyer, and out of this church and running to Dalton before they could catch up.

But when she turned to face forward again, her hope shattered. A woman stood in front of her, blocking the exit.

Esther stopped dead. The woman moved toward her.

"Stay away!" Esther shouted. "Don't kill me!"

"Esther, are you okay?" the woman asked. She had stopped advancing. "Who's trying to kill you?"

"They are... They, they..." Esther put her hands on top of her head. "Wait. Abby? Is that you?"

It was the small red-headed woman who had introduced herself as Pastor Teddy's assistant on the day of her interview. Her ghostly white face was bunched up in an expression of confusion.

"We have to go!" Esther cried. She ran to Abby and grabbed her shoulders. "They killed Brittany!"

"Who?"

"Good job catching her!" The last hooded figure said as he approached. "Wait. What are *you* doing here?"

Esther turned to see the man just a few feet away from her.

"You're not supposed to be here," the man said to Abby.

"Who the fuck are you?" Abby said. She took a step back. Esther stepped back with her.

The man removed his hood.

"Chad?" Abby exclaimed.

Esther caught the woman as her knees buckled at the sight of the man's face.

"It's me," Chad said. He held his arms out as if to put himself on display. "Your best friend!"

"No!" Abby shouted. "It's impossible!"

"Oh, it's possible," a deep, familiar voice boomed.

Pastor Teddy moved to stand beside Chad. If Abby's knees had buckled at the sight of her best friend, they gave away entirely at the appearance of the pastor. His cloak had been completely removed so that his black shirt and preacher's collar were visible. His white beard glistened with sweat. He was breathing heavily.

"Dad?" Abby said. "How...?"

"Hello, daughter," the pastor said.

Esther looked at Abby, confused. "Daughter?"

"Yes," Abby answered. "I must... I must be hallucinating."

Pastor Teddy's chest bounced with his laughter. The sanctuary seamed to shake along with it, as if an earthquake had joined in on the joke.

"That's an understatement," he said. His voice became even deeper than before. It had a new quality to it, too, as if it was layered, like multiple voices speaking at once. It also seemed amplified somehow. "You should have stayed in bed with that girlfriend of yours. This church is no longer your concern. You have no business here."

Esther grabbed Abby's arm and squeezed. "I'm sorry, Abby, but your father killed Brittany."

"No. He didn't." Abby said confidently. "And that's not my father."

"But you just said..." Esther looked back and forth between the two of them. "What do you mean, he's not your father?"

"I mean exactly that. This is *not* my father. My dad is dead."

"He doesn't look dead to me!"

"Well, he is. Believe me! And it's my fault."

"That's right," Pastor Teddy said coolly. "It was your fault. Tell her why."

Abby's shoulders slumped. "I... I told my dad about Libby. She's my girlfriend. He didn't take the news well."

Chad giggled.

"But he came around," Abby continued. "He told me he loved me and that I had opened his eyes. He said he was going to make some changes around here. So, the church board had a meeting." Tears poured down her cheeks. "My dad died in that meeting. A man named Victor shot and killed him."

Chad exploded with laughter.

"Shut up, Chad!" Abby shouted. "You died in that meeting, too!"

Chad fell silent.

The thing that looked like Pastor Teddy took a step forward. "She speaks the truth, from a certain point of view. But Abby, here I am. And I wanted to tell you, I've changed my mind. The board and the other pastors were correct. I was letting my feelings for you allow sin into this camp. Your sin. The wages of sin is death. And now I'm dead."

"I'm dead, too?" Chad asked.

"Yes, Abby's sin killed you, too. I'm sorry."

Abby's body trembled. Her breathing increased.

"That's how I know you're not my dad!" she said through gritted teeth. "My dad would never say such hurtful things to me. He told me he planned on staying here as pastor and making some changes. He told me there would be a vote, and if it didn't go his way, he would step down as pastor. But it *did* go his way, and he was killed because of it."

Pastor Teddy burst out laughing. His guffawing was joined by the high-pitched, rowdy cackling of many others. More hooded individuals strode into view and stood behind the pastor like a church choir, except the only ensemble performance this choir would be taking part in would be the execution of Esther and Abby. Her knees weakened.

I can do all things through—

"In the name of Christ. Reveal yourself!" Abby commanded abruptly.

Esther looked at her with wide eyes. *Is she performing an exorcism?*

Abby looked different now. She stood defiant, in opposition to whatever evil was before her. She looked like a warrior princess in tight-fitting jeans and a tucked-in Deftones T-shirt. A fire raged within her eyes.

Her sudden confidence was contagious. Esther stood up straighter and balled her fists.

We're performing an exorcism.

Upon Abby's command, the choir of evil started swaying back and forth as if they could hear music than no one else could hear.

Pastor Teddy growled. The hooded choir growled along with him. The guttural sounds made Esther think of a pack of wild animals. Thick strings of clear saliva dripped from the pastor's mouth and travelled down his beard. Droplets of drool flew from his face with each exhalation.

Without knowing exactly what she was doing, Esther moved beside Abby and yelled at the pastor, "In the name of Christ. Reveal yourself!"

If two of you on earth agree about anything you ask…

At this, Pastor Teddy let out a shriek. His followers howled like wolves. The pastor raised his hands in front of his face. His fingertips split as sharp claws grew from them, black like obsidian. Those claws scratched at his own face. The skin split and tore away as if it had barely been hanging on in the first place. The pastor grabbed his beard and yanked. What patches of flesh remained now pulled away like tender meat falling from a bone. His entire face slid off like a cheap Halloween mask. He held his white beard within a clawed fist, mutilated flesh clinging to it. Casually, he threw it. It landed on the floor in front of Esther's feet with a wet thump.

"What the hell is happening?" Esther asked.

Abby reached over and grabbed her hand. "I think it's doing what we asked it to."

"Maybe we shouldn't have asked."

From the bloody, mangled area that had once been the demon's face, a protrusion grew. It was a new face. Grayish black hair covered it. A wet black nose decorated the end of the protrusion. The lump of new flesh ripped down the middle into two distinct parts, an upper and lower jaw. Razor sharp teeth lined the inside. A long red tongue licked at the teeth.

The same coarse hair began growing on the pastor's arms. As the hair grew, so did the man's frame. He had already been large to begin with, but now his muscles and stature were such that his clothes tore. His shirt ripped, but the preacher's collar remained. It stretched around the thickening neck to the brink of popping, but it refused to pop. His pants tore as new, massive calf muscles formed. His shoes popped open as growing flesh emerged from them. Long black claws like the claws of the hands shot out of the monster's newly formed toes.

"Is that…" Esther began. "Did he just turn into a…"

"A werewolf," Abby stated matter-of-factly, as if she had been expecting it all along. She looked at the preacher's collar, which still circled the creature's neck like a dog collar. "A fucking wolf in shepherd's clothing."

The wolf turned its head up and howled. The crowd behind it did the same. As they howled, they too began to transform. Their bodies appeared to boil within their cloaks. They jerked this way and that. The howling died down as, one by one, each brown cloak dropped to the ground as if its wearer had disappeared. Steam and a strange glow seeped out from underneath the brown cloaks, which looked like large anthills littering the sanctuary floor behind the werewolf. Esther imagined a clump of melted and congealed human flesh within them.

Whatever remained of the bodies under the cloaks began to move. The mounds of fabric fell away as creatures crawled out from beneath them. The creatures resembled wolves, but not wolves of this world. They stood on all fours, and their faces resembled that of the werewolf. Patches of hair across their bodies had burned away. Smoke poured out of cracks in their skin that spiderwebbed across the entirety of their bodies. Orange-red light shone through the cracks as if their insides were made of molten lava. They raised their heads up and howled. The noise echoed throughout the sanctuary.

"This is my church now," the werewolf said over the bellowing of its followers. A large, tooth-filled grin inside its snout. The smile looked unnatural on such a visage. The beast's words were accompanied by a continual snarl that seemed to emanate from deep within its chest.

"Why did you care so much for a man that doesn't understand you?" the monster said. When it talked, it's snout scrunched up, as if every word he spoke pissed him off. "He was no ally. He didn't care about any of the things that matter to you. Believe me. I know how he thought. I put thoughts just like his in the minds of millions over millennia."

Abby shook her head. Her red hair danced.

"I cared..." she said, taking a step toward the beast, "and I still care, because he was my dad! So you can back off with your ideological bullshit."

Esther was in awe. If Abby was at all afraid, she wasn't showing it. She, on the other hand, was starting to lose her briefly borrowed confidence. It had begun leaking away as she had watched a man transform into a werewolf. Her mind was full of thoughts, but there was one thought that was the loudest.

Dalton was telling the truth. The whole truth.

The werewolf scratched its left shoulder with its claws.

"You are a kink in my plan, Abby." it said. "You are also correct, by the way. Your dad had decided to take this church in a new, more loving direction, or quit if he was voted out. I was impressed, and also upset. He was thinking outside this church-shaped box for the first time in a long time. I had to stop him. So, I whispered something into Victor's ear and—*boom!* Dead daddy."

"And dead Chad!" the wolf that had once looked like Chad added with a growl.

The werewolf backhanded the wolf that stood beside him. It squealed and backed into the pack, disappearing into obscurity.

Up until this point, Esther had dealt with so many conflicting thoughts and emotions that she had forgotten about escaping. Listening to the conversation between Abby and the werewolf had actually given her body and brain time to get back on the same page. They both agreed on something. It was time to run!

Esther turned and sprinted toward the exit, pulling Abby along with her. She didn't turn to see if the wolves would give chase. There was no need. She knew that they had.

Esther burst through the exit with Abby in tow. They were now back in the long hallway with all the metal doors.

She made for the foyer, but something told her she wouldn't make it. Her bare feet slapped on the floor as she ran past doors on both sides. Wolf paws clapped against the floor not far behind her. It sounded like she was trying to outrun a stampede.

She was no longer pulling Abby along. Abby, obviously having realized that bravado alone wouldn't defeat a pack of deadly demon wolves, was keeping pace beside her. They still held hands.

"We can't outrun them!" Abby shouted.

"What do we do?" Esther shouted back.

Sharp teeth bit at her heel. She fell to the floor. Intense pain shot up her left leg.

I send you out as lambs in the midst of wolves.

CHANGE (IN THE HOUSE OF GOD) PART 2

2022

Pastor Teddy pushed the door to the conference room open and forced himself to walk back inside. He acted calm and confident, but his stomach churned. He wasn't bluffing; he really was ready to step down as pastor if he was voted out, but he wanted so badly to remain. He knew he could find meaning outside the walls of a church building—after all, he was cognizant that the church was actually made of people, not bricks and buildings. But his usefulness had been tied to this place for so long, it was hard for him to imagine walking away. He sat in his seat at the head of the conference table and looked around the room.

"I'm ready to find out my fate." He said. "How do we do this?"

Of course, Victor was the one to speak up.

"To keep things anonymous, we wrote our votes on pieces of paper. Votes for *remain* or *remove*. All the pieces have been placed in this coffee mug." Victor slid the mug across the surface of the table. Pastor Teddy caught it securely in the palm of his hand. "Per our bylaws, there can be only one dissenting vote. Meaning two votes for you to step down is enough to have you removed as pastor."

"I know the bylaws," Pastor Teddy said. "I have participated in a vote before." He looked at Victor and saw acknowledgment in his eyes. He reached inside the coffee mug and pulled out a tiny piece of ripped paper.

"Vote one," the pastor said. He looked at the paper and read aloud, "Remain."

The knot inside his stomach loosened just a little. He had expected an immediate vote for removal. This was encouraging, but he didn't allow himself to hope too much. He had probably just pulled out Chad's vote first. All the rest would most likely be for removal. He looked at Chad, and the young man winked at him. He reached inside the mug for a second time. When he looked at the small piece of paper, his chest tightened.

"Remove."

No one said a word in response. Pastor Teddy honestly couldn't remember another time he had been in a room full of so much tension. It felt as though the will of God was being decided by these men in this room, right now. He laughed internally.

God's perfect will, he thought. *Squeezed inside a church coffee mug.*

"One more is all it takes," Victor blurted out.

"At least try to hide your smugness," Chad snapped.

Victor opened his mouth to defend himself. Before he could, Pastor Teddy read another vote.

"Remain."

Sighs of relief washed across the room. The pastor tried to gauge how many of the voters seemed relieved.

Is it all of them?

It was impossible to tell. He pulled another vote from the cup.

"Remain."

Chad actually cheered. The rest of the staff remained more composed than the worship pastor, but there were no obvious signs of disapproval on any of their faces, other than Victor's, of course.

"Remain."

"Remain."

"Remain."

To Pastor Teddy's disbelief, every sheet of paper he pulled out said the same thing. It seemed that more people were willing to follow where Jesus was leading the church than he had initially thought.

I should have known these men were willing. They just needed me to take the first step of faith.

He continued to read votes. To Victor's obvious dissatisfaction, all were for *remain.*

"One final vote," the pastor announced. He didn't want to admit it to himself, but he now had a good feeling about the whole situation. Everyone in attendance leaned forward in their seats. Pastor Teddy felt as though he was about to announce the winner of *American Idol* or something. He pulled out the final piece of paper from the mug and held it in his hand.

Your will be done.

He read the last vote, not out loud, but to himself. He looked around the room. Nobody seemed to be breathing. He looked at Victor. The man's face was contorted, as if awaiting the final result was causing him physical pain.

This isn't just a vote to this man. He wants me to be found guilty of something.

Pastor Teddy's eyes watered as he read the vote out loud, "Remain."

He squeezed the paper tightly in his palm. He stood up—he couldn't help it. His mind was telling him to act cool, but internally he wanted to celebrate. He couldn't have forced a frown on his face if he wanted to.

The others in attendance all stood and cheered, clapping and patting each other on the back. The conference room now resembled a party room more than a place for serious meetings.

"No!" Victor screamed.

Instantly, the atmosphere of the room changed from party central to more like a courtroom.

"We can't let this happen!" Victor shouted frantically. He was looking at the other men in the room, imploring them with his words, eyes and body language to see reason. It was as if he was trying to make eye contact with everyone in the room at once—everyone except Pastor Teddy.

"He's polluting God's house!" he said, pointing at the pastor but not looking at him. "It's our job as leaders to put a stop to this!" His pointer finger traveled around the room, stopping for a moment on each man in attendance. Pastor Teddy had never noticed before, but Victor's finger was crooked, as if it had once been broken. Also, its knuckle was humongous, like a swollen Adam's apple. "We are overseers!" Victor continued. "The vote must be challenged."

"Calm down," said a man named Ernest, who had remained silent until now. He had gray hair, a mustache and a very serious demeanor. He looked like a cowboy. He actually did wear a cowboy hat whenever he wasn't under the church's roof. He was an elder, and had been one since the foundation of the church. When he spoke, even Victor paid attention. He remained seated beside Pastor Teddy.

"Please sit," he said, motioning to the chairs around the table.

Anyone who was standing obeyed immediately.

"Obviously, I voted for Pastor Teddy to stay," he said. "Now, I'm as old school as I am old." A few people around the table chuckled. "I don't know what to think about all these youngsters today, with all their genders and such.

Seems like a bunch of craziness to me." He paused and took a deep breath. Everyone was hanging on his every word, and he knew it. "But I do know what to think about our pastor. He's a good man. Now Victor—" he looked at the deacon, "—you cling to the Bible so tight, and yet you don't. Ain't a one of us that actually lives how that book says. Don't know if we could if we wanted to. God might be the same yesterday, today and forever, but we aren't. Times are a-changing. And when you say you know exactly what Jesus would do in the year of our Lord 2023... it just shows me how profoundly ignorant you are. What would Jesus Facebook? What would Jesus tweet? I don't know. But I sure as heck think it would be mixed with a lot more love and patience than us Christians of today show." He looked away from Victor and turned his attention toward Pastor Teddy. "Young man, you are my pastor and the shepherd of this flock. I trust you and your heart for God. Therefore, I'm willing to give this new direction a try. I'm sure, after a lifetime of living, I've gotten a few things wrong." He leaned closer to the pastor. "But remember, I'll have my eye on you. And God does, too."

Pastor Teddy grinned. "I wouldn't want it any other way." He reached over and placed a hand on the man's shoulder. "And Ernest, thank you."

Something inside of Pastor Teddy clicked, as if a missing piece of the puzzle that represented how he saw God had been moved to the correct space. The puzzle would never be completed, at least not in this lifetime, but that didn't mean it wasn't worth attempting to assemble it. Just working on it made him a better person. He would spend the rest of his life doing so. The problem was, he didn't have much life left to live.

A sound attracted the attention of everyone in the room. Though it was familiar, hearing it here stripped it of its familiarity. Pastor Teddy had heard this noise thousands of times before. He owned multiple guns. He had a membership to the local gun range, which wasn't far from the church, and went there often. He found it relaxing to shoot off a few rounds at paper targets. It took his mind off the stress of running a church as big as Hillside Community Church. When he was shooting, he had to focus, which took his focus off the bad things in his life, like his workload, and other people's problems, and, most importantly, the death of his wife. Every bullet fired down range made a similar sound to the sound he just heard. At the range, though, he was usually wearing ear protection. Also, the noise was never followed by pain in his chest.

Am I having a heart attack?

He looked down. There was a hole in his shirt. Blood started to saturate the area around it. He looked away, not wanting to see what he was seeing. His attention was taken by something just as disturbing.

Victor was standing. He held a Glock 19 in his hand. The gun was aimed at the pastor.

It fired a second time. A 9mm shell casing hit the wooden table and rolled on its surface until it became caught in the armpit of the Jesus carving in its center.

There was a third shot. Pastor Teddy braced himself, but didn't feel its impact. He had expected pain, but the only pain had been from the first two impacts, which had felt like someone had thrown stones at him.

Let him without sin cast the first stone.

Victor grabbed at his chest. He flew back into his seat, hard. It dawned on Pastor Teddy that the reason he hadn't felt another stone throw was because the third shot hadn't been directed at him.

Ernest was standing, holding a Kimber 1911 in his hands.

"Someone help the pastor!" he shouted.

Hands grabbed at Pastor Teddy's chest. Some placed pressure on his wounds, some were simply placed there to pray for him. All were trying to help.

"We're losing him!" someone shouted.

Pastor Teddy wondered why the person had said that. He was fine. He was still sitting up in his chair. He should be fine. He was just a little sleepy. He wished they would all give him some space. Instead, they crowded him even more.

"Stay with us!" someone said. "Has anyone called 911?"

Pastor Teddy forced his sleepy eyes open. It was the most difficult thing he had ever done. It would take something extraordinary to get them to remain open. He looked past the frantic men trying their best to help him. Behind them, the dead body of Victor sat motionless in a chair. A hole in his chest.

Poor bastard, Teddy thought.

He was about to give in to the tugging at his eyelids when something extraordinary happened. The dead body in the chair started to move. Victor stood. His motions were jerky, as if he was having a hard time controlling his lifeless limbs.

Hey. He's moving, Pastor Teddy tried to say. The words were in his mind, but he couldn't get them out. *Watch out. He's got the gun!*

The sound of gunfire echoed throughout the room. It was so loud it made Pastor Teddy wake up. He watched in horror as Ernest fell to the floor. A hole that matched the ones in his own chest was visible right between Ernest's eyes.

More shots rang out. More men fell. Victor's movements were still jerky, but he moved at a speed that was almost superhuman.

"Get him!" someone shouted.

Those that had not been shot ran toward Victor, but he ducked and disappeared under the table.

"He went under the table!"

As quick as lightning, Victor popped up beside the pastor. He had tossed his Glock and now held Ernest's Kimber.

"There he is!" Chad exclaimed.

Those were the last words he ever said. His head exploded as a bullet ripped through his skull.

"No!" Pastor Teddy managed to scream.

Not long after, every man in the room, aside from the pastor and Victor, was dead. Adrenaline rushed through Pastor Teddy's veins. Somehow, he found the will to stand. It was too late to save his employees—his friends—but he had to stop Victor. Also...

Abby, his mind screamed. *Got to live, for Abby.*

Abby was in the building. If he didn't end Victor's killing spree here and now, there was no telling how many more lives would be extinguished.

He rushed at the man, pushing rolling chairs aside as he did so. Victor smiled and threw away the gun. He opened his arms as if he were welcoming an old friend. Pastor Teddy crashed into him, and the pair landed on the table. The pastor was on top, slamming his fists into Victor's face. Victor laughed. Teddy could see blood tracing his teeth.

"You're dying," Victor cackled. "Your punches are like a pillow fight."

Pastor Teddy stopped punching and decided to try and strangle Victor instead. He squeezed Victor's neck as hard as he could, though that wasn't very hard at all. His taunting had been accurate. Teddy was dying. Blood leaked out of him. His vision blurred.

Jesus. I'm ready to come home.

The table split down the middle and collapsed. Victor's back slammed onto the floor. Teddy landed on top of him, his face pressed so close to Victor's that their noses were touching. Teddy jerked his head back and squeezed harder at the man's throat.

I will finish this! he thought.

Through blurred vision he saw something unbelievable. Two antlers shot out of the top of Victor's head. From his face, which was still very close to his own, a protrusion grew. Grayish black hair covered it. The growing lump of new flesh ripped into two distinct parts, making an upper and lower jaw. Teeth grew on the inside.

"What the..." Pastor Teddy said. He was once again fully aware. He knew he would die soon, but whatever was happening was too confusing for him to go just yet. The neck he was currently trying to crush expanded, enlarging so rapidly he was forced to let go. Coarse hair covered it.

Two wings with feathers as long as Pastor Teddy's forearms rocketed out from Victor's back. They looked as big as Teddy had always imagined an angel's wings would be. An angel's wings would be white, though. These wings were brown, like an owl's. They wrapped themselves around the pastor's body as if he was an owlet in a nest. Pastor Teddy's world went dark. He wondered briefly if it was because he had finally died—but that was not the case. Not yet. He was within the all-encompassing embrace of a beast of some kind. It had been hideous within the light of the room. Now, within its embrace, all he could make out of the creature were two glowing red eyes. The beast squeezed him tight.

"You built this church on top of *my* ashes," it growled. "And on top of *my* bones. I will not let you turn it into anything other than my home."

As if a light switch had been flipped, Pastor Teddy could see again. He rolled away as, abruptly, the beast stood. Teddy landed on his back, in the exact location where the creature had been lying a second ago. The monster towered over him. Its antlers scraped the ceiling of the conference room.

"You demon!" Pastor Teddy exclaimed.

The monster cracked its neck and then transformed yet again. This time, it shrank instead of growing. Every mutation and demonic trait it had gained now folded back into its body. The antlers, wings, and snout all collapsed until they were no more. In a matter of seconds, the monster appeared human once more. Pastor Teddy looked up into Victor's eyes.

"Demon?" Victor said. He held out his arms and appeared to study them. "You hit the crucifixion nail on the head. Now, if you'll excuse me... I have a church to shepherd." He reached down and grabbed both sides of Pastor Teddy's head. "And a daughter to let down."

He opened his mouth wide—wider than ought to be possible. The corners of his mouth began to tear, and then something wet and slimy began crawling out of Victor's gullet. It moved slowly out from between the man's pink lips, like a worm emerging from damp earth. It resembled a centipede, without any legs. It was coated in a tar-like black substance. Even before its back end was all the way out of Victor's mouth, its front was slithering between Pastor Teddy's lips.

The pastor couldn't breathe. The thing was pushing its way down his windpipe. He was being forced to swallow something he knew would kill him. He watched with crossed eyes as its front end disappeared into his mouth. The creature burrowed its way into him, making his body its home. Teddy's stomach tightened. Every muscle he had tightened. His body seemed to understand that a foreign invader was inside and wanted to collapse in on itself, just to kill it. Suddenly, his gunshot wounds were of no consequence. Whatever was happening to him now made being shot seem like nothing more than a mosquito bite.

"Oh God!" he cried out.

His insides churned. The thing was moving inside him. It was crawling up, towards his brain. He tried to move, but he couldn't. He had lost all control of his body functions. All he could do now was think. Think of all the mistakes he had made. Think about how he had let his church get to a place where *this* could happen within its walls. Think about his daughter, and how he had let her down.

———

My dad and my best friend were the only ones to actually die that day. The only facts I know are from what the police report says, but in my nightmares I see it all, I feel it all. I am my father when I dream. I watch my church fall apart, and my entire flock perishes at the hands of a wolf that I allowed to remain.

— Abby

SEPARATION ANXIETY

"Get it off me!" Esther screamed.

When the fastest of the demon wolves had caught up with her, its bite on her ankle had made her spin around and fall to the ground. She now sat on her butt and kicked at the wolf's snout with her bare feet. The other members of the pack were only a few yards away. The orange glow that emanated from within the creature's cracked skin crawled up the walls.

Sharp teeth chomped at her toes. She watched in disbelief as her two smallest digits were severed by the beast's fangs, then disappeared down the monster's gullet. Blood squirted out of the nubs where they had been moments ago. She could see her toe bones. Esther screamed in anger, more than agony, and used her heel to deliver a kick to the beast's face. Blood got in its eyes, and the wolf recoiled. A second wolf took its place and lunged for Esther's legs.

The creature bit down on air as Esther was pulled to safety. Abby had grabbed onto her arm and yanked her through a doorway. A metal door slammed shut just as the wolf that had eaten her toes lunged for her. Esther heard a loud thud and the door rattled on its hinges. The sound of claws scratching at the bottom of the door made Esther think of fingernails running down a chalkboard.

"Thank you, Abby," she said through heavy breathing. She sat on the ground, holding onto her bloody foot.

"Anytime," Abby responded. She sat with her back to the door, holding it shut.

The scratching at the door didn't last long. The growls of their pursuers eventually died down.

"You wanna open the door and check?" Esther asked.

"Hell no."

"Where are we, anyways?"

Abby pointed down the dark hall behind Esther. Every fifteen feet, emergency light fixtures created pockets of visibility. "I know where this leads. There's an exit this way. Out the door at the end of this hall is an indoor playground. On the other side of that is the children's church. There's a back door in the kid's church that leads outside."

Esther wanted to ask Abby how she knew so much about this place, but then it occurred to her. "Preacher's kids know the church better than anyone," she said as she ripped the left sleeve off her shirt and wrapped it tightly around her injured foot.

"We do," Abby agreed. "Can you walk?"

"Yes," Esther answered defiantly. She struggled to stand, but managed it. "Let's go."

***

Dalton was halfway across the cavernous foyer before he paid any attention to where he was headed. He dove behind a couch and peeked over the back of it at the front door of the church to see if the witch had followed him. His heart thudded in his chest, as if he had run much farther than he actually had.

"Why won't she stay dead?"

Before he was even born, this demon had appeared at the foot of his parents' marriage bed to terrify them. Dalton had often wondered if her witch-like appearance was due to his parents deep-seated fears of the occult. They were products of the eighties. Satanic panic had taken root in them and never stopped growing. Dalton hadn't been allowed to watch most television shows or movies when he was a kid. He was only allowed to listen to Christian music. His kid brain had thought that each and every secular music album could be played in reverse to reveal hidden Satanic messages. He could recall overhearing his parents speak of conspiracy theories of child sacrifice and ritualistic mutilation enacted in the name of Satan, always in the next town over. Because of this, Dalton had always felt he was more prone than others to inject spiritual activity or demonic influence into the most mundane of situations. Still, whether real or metaphorical, he was certain that he had defeated this demon years ago, when he had spent the night in his father's church. He had faced his fears. He had faced his family's darkness, and the witch had been defeated. She was swallowed up within an all-consuming fire that had also consumed his father's church. Its ashes, as well as the remains of the witch, were probably mixed into the very foundations on which this new church had been built.

Dalton watched the front door for a long time. Thankfully, the door remained closed. No witch entered the premises. Still, he was certain that he was not alone.

As his breathing returned to just about normal, his thoughts returned to Esther. Whatever was happening, he was sure that she was in the middle of it. The witch always messed with the ones he loved. She messed with his family. Although he and Esther were not yet married, she was family.

Should we get married? The thought seemed to come out of nowhere. His thoughts had been doing that a lot lately.

The witch had mentioned a generational curse. Dalton remembered his dad preaching sermons about generational curses. It made sense that the witch had been a part of the Folmer family as far back as any Folmer existed. This was the very reason Dalton had decided never to have kids. His brother James had been supportive of the decision, but had also told him that he might be giving the witch power again, with his fear. James had gone in the opposite direction and had had four kids.

Dalton stood and took in his surroundings. He felt small, not only because of the enormity of the room, but because this was the first time he had been inside a church building in at least twenty years. People he met with occasionally encouraged his spiritual journey and even prayed with him. Esther was a part of that community. It was church. But the meetings were usually spontaneous and always somewhere that was *not* an evangelical church building.

He looked down at his feet and, in spite of everything, he chuckled. He was missing his right shoe. Its absence revealed a dirty white sock with a large hole in it. His big toe stuck out of the hole. He wiggled it and then slid his socked foot across the slick floor of the foyer.

I wonder what part of my father's church I would be standing in now, if it were still here?

He shook away his nostalgia and walked toward a hallway lined with metal doors. He didn't have time to linger on the past. He didn't even have time to question what was happening. All he knew was that he had been in a similar situation before and had come out the victor. He had saved his little brother. This time, he would save Esther. He would once again shut down whatever evil had grown like a cancer, in the name of Christendom. He had grown to believe that most of the time when someone spoke of fighting a spiritual battle, the battle was actually nothing more than a made-up fairy tale in their head, to help them cope with whatever real-world problem they were dealing with. Yet, he knew in his soul that, on occasion, the battles were real. He didn't want this fight to be real, but he would fight as if it were. Tonight he would wrestle with flesh and blood and the rulers of the darkness of this world, all at the same time.

"Esther!" he whisper-shouted as he walked down the hallway. "Esther, where are you?" He passed door after door. Each had a plaque on top, labeling the room or area it led to. Passing through any door would be nothing more than a guess. His thought was to find the sanctuary, or possibly the pastor's office. He considered those to be his most educated guesses as to Esther's whereabouts. Before either of those options became available, a new possibility enticed him.

"Child development center," he read aloud from the plaque above a door with a metal push bar dividing its mid-center. The door had deep scratch marks at its base. He had seen the CDC from outside. It was the part of the building that had the transparent dome on its roof.

"That's where I saw the crazy lights," he said to himself. "Something bad is happening in there." His jaw tightened and he shook his head. "And I bet Esther is right in the middle of it."

Without wasting a moment, he pushed the door open and stepped through. The door shut behind him. Dalton found himself at the beginning of yet another long hallway. It was dark, but emergency lighting lit the way. He felt for a light switch panel but found none.

Slowly, he made his way down the hall. There was something wet on the floor, which soaked into his sock as he walked. He stooped to check it out. In the semidarkness he saw a trail of dark red blood. Small, bloody footprints stretched down the hall as if showing the way. The trail went on for as far as Dalton could see. Looking behind him, he noticed that the bloody impressions originated at the door. Usually, blood on the ground would be a good indicator that one should turn back, but his duty was to follow the trail like a hunter tracking a kill. Instead, though, he hoped to save whoever he found at the end of the trail—especially if that someone was Esther. The size of the prints did look like a match for her foot size. The thought of his partner being injured and having lost this much blood worried him. He allowed the worry to push him on instead of freeze him into inaction.

I'm coming, Esther.

He followed the trail. Interestingly, there seemed to be two sets of prints.

Did Esther make a friend? he wondered. *Or has she been captured?*

He increased his pace, occasionally passing doors on either side. These doors were wooden and familiar from his school days. On the other side of them were almost assuredly classrooms for differing age groups. Each door had the name of a teacher printed on it in colorful bubble letters. From behind the doors he heard noises that did not belong in such innocent places. Noises of torture and violation. Children screamed. He heard chants that were deep and guttural. They made him think of demonic rituals. Through unfortunate experience, Dalton knew to ignore the noise. This trick had been used on him once before, a long time ago, when he had been only thirteen years old. The witch had used the tactic in order to delay him and ultimately try to stop him from accomplishing his mission of saving his brother. It had almost worked. This time, he would ignore whatever he heard or saw, until he found Esther.

The door at the end of the hallway was fast approaching. It was metal, exactly like the one he had come through moments ago, minus the weird scratches at the base.

As he passed a final classroom on his left, the door burst open, as if inviting him inside. In his peripheral vision he saw a teenage boy sitting slumped over in a large chair. The witch was standing behind the chair.

Ignore it.

But something about the vision was too difficult to ignore. There were wires and tubes connected to the chair and to the boy. There was also a sort of metal hat on his head, which looked like a big, upturned salad bowl. Two thick wires were connected to it. The child's hands and feet were bound to the chair with leather straps.

None of this surprised Dalton. He had half expected to see this at some point. What he was looking at was a perfect recreation of his friend Kirk's death on the night he had spent in his father's church when he was thirteen. There was the electric chair straight out of a movie, big and brown, with a tall backrest. The wood looked old and splintered. The leather straps that held the kid to the chair were thick and padded. The witch's hands rested upon a large, gray lever.

Her face was obscured within the shadows of her tattered hood, just as she had worn that night. Her eyes glowed as red as ever.

"Ready to let another one die, Dalton?" she screeched.

Dalton did not enter the room. He knew how this ended. Remaining in the hall, he said, "I am my brother's keeper," with a calmness in his voice that surprised even him. "But I also can't save them all." He leaned forward and grabbed the door handle. "Flip the switch," he said.

She cackled and obeyed.

Electricity coursed through the boy. Sparks flew and his body convulsed as smoke rose from his cooking skin. It was all exactly as Dalton remembered it. Every gruesome detail was the same—with one exception. This was what had caused Dalton to pause and take in the scene, in spite of knowing better. This time, the boy in the chair was not Kirk. It was a thirteen-year-old Dalton.

Dalton pulled the door closed, shaking his head. He could still hear the crackle of electricity. The smell of his own tender flesh cooking followed him as he followed the bloody footprints along the hall to the metal door. On the ground next to the door was a body that hadn't been there before. Dalton knelt down to examine it.

"Kirk?"

Kirk's dead body lay there with a needle sticking out of a big purple vein. There was a pool of vomit on the floor next to his face, and more of it was crusted on his chapped lips.

"Why didn't you call me?" Dalton said to the dead body, even though he knew it wasn't really there. "I would have helped any way I could have."

He waited for the dead body to spring back to life and start blaming him for Kirk's death. Any moment now, it would animate and start screaming about how hot Hell was.

It didn't happen, though. The body just lay rotting. Dalton thought it was actually scarier that way.

He stood and pushed open the metal door, leaving Kirk behind to step into whatever madness awaited him next.

***

Esther looked up. The moon shone brightly through the transparent dome above her. Silvery light washed over the indoor playground. The place was cleaner than most playgrounds. The equipment was impressive. It looked fun—fun enough that if Esther had found herself here under different circumstances, she would have had a hard time not climbing to the top of one of the towers and sliding down one of the many twisting slides. Fun is fun, even in your forties.

Abby called to Esther from halfway across the room, "Are you coming?"

"Sorry," Esther responded. She walked with a slight limp through the playground equipment to reach Abby. The floor was soft, covered with some sort of thick padding, to prevent kids that fell off the monkey bars from breaking their necks. "I've never seen such an impressive playground. And indoors, too."

"It's pretty common nowadays," Abby told her. "In bigger churches, at least. The dome lets light in, so it feels like outside. But being on the inside of the building keeps the kids much more safe from things like kidnappings or shootings."

The logic made sense. But something about how blasé Abby had said it made Esther sick. She ducked and followed Abby under a tiny wooden bridge that connected one tower to another. There were many similar bridges that stretched across the area. The towers looked like tree houses, covered with fake tree branches and greenery. The whole playground reminded Esther of an Ewok village. She could imagine cute, but still savage, little creatures traversing the bridges.

She heard footfalls on the bridge above her head.

Was that my imagination?

"Did you hear that?" Abby asked.

Both women darted out from under the bridge and turned to look up at it. There was nothing there.

"I'm afraid a wolf is gonna jump out at me every time I turn around," Esther said.

"I feel the same way."

After a few moments, Esther asked, "What's really going on here?"

"You wouldn't believe me if I told you," Abby answered.

"Try me. I haven't had the best church experiences in my life, but I've never had anything like this happen. My boyfriend, on the other hand... let's just say he's been in this kind of situation before."

"Really?" Abby said incredulously. "What's his name?"

"You two actually have something in common. He was a preacher's kid, too. At a church that used to sit on this very property."

Abby stopped dead. Her white skin somehow turned whiter, like a ghost. She reached out and grabbed Esther by the shoulders, shaking her hard. "Did his dad's church burn down?" Her face came very close to Esther's. "Did he ever talk about a witch with antlers that rides around on a headless deer?" She squeezed Esther's shoulders so tight that it hurt. Her breath was hot against Esther's face. "Is your boyfriend's name Dalton?"

Esther pulled herself away from Abby's grip. How did this young woman know these things? What was going on here? More information was needed, but before she had a chance to answer *yes*, her partner's name was in fact, Dalton, and *yes*, he often spoke of the witch who rode a headless deer, and *yes*, his father's church had burnt to the ground, a high pitched fit of giggling caught her attention.

"What was that?"

Esther pointed. "Over there! In the tree house."

Abby looked where Esther was pointing. "I don't see anything."

"Keep looking. I saw something move in there."

"What did it look like?"

"I don't know," Esther admitted. "It looked... It kinda looked like a kid."

"A kid?" Abby asked. "There's no way."

"There he is again!" Esther pointed at a small black boy who could be no older than five. He was wearing blue shorts and a *Jurassic World* tank top shirt with a picture of a velociraptor on it. The boy stood motionless on the wooden bridge. "Tell me you see him too?"

"Oh, I see him," Abby said. "He's cute."

"Totally." Esther agreed. "Totally cute. But... is it okay if I say..."

"He's creepy," Abby admitted in a hushed tone. "He's also a little creepy-looking."

Abby took a step toward the child. Esther hung back, not wanting to frighten him. Abby waved. "Hi," she said in a high-pitched voice. "My name is Abby. And this is my friend Esther."

Esther waved and smiled.

"Are you okay?" Abby asked. "How long have you been here?"

The boy remained silent. Esther couldn't tell for sure, but it looked like he had been crying.

"What's your name?" Abby asked.

No response. Abby looked back at Esther. Esther took that as her cue to try something. She took a few steps forward.

"This playground is just awesome," she said. "I bet you know all the fun stuff to do here. Would it be okay if I climbed up there and played, too?"

At this, the boy smiled a big smile. But it didn't ease any of the tension from the situation. The smile seemed unnatural, having appeared too quickly on the kid's face. He had gone from upset to ecstatic in no time. And the smile continued to grow.

"Okay..." Esther said sheepishly. "Okay, then. I'm coming up."

She moved to a winding staircase that appeared to lead up to one of the treehouse towers connected to the bridge the kid was on. Just before she reached the stairs, she heard a humming sound. It was coming from the child. She paused to listen. He was humming a melody that she knew well. Most people that grew up in church would have known it. She sang the accompanying words in her head as she hummed along.

Jesus loves the little children. All the children of the world. Red, brown, yellow, black, and white, they are precious in his sight. Jesus loves the little children of the world.

Esther continued humming as she made her way up the stairs. She took them slowly. Her foot actually didn't hurt nearly as bad as she thought it should. Still, climbing stairs reminded her that she was wounded, and humming the lullaby soothed her nerves a bit. This night had gone nothing like she had expected. Yes, she had had a slight suspicion that the women of this church were in danger. But honestly, she had just thought they were leaving due to evangelical sexism in the name of Jesus. Like when a pastor had an affair with a woman and then the woman was shunned, while the man was forgiven and then rehabilitated back into leadership, now with a powerful testimony. She never would have guessed that the women were being murdered.

Did Dalton actually suspect this?

She wanted nothing more than to reach this child and follow Abby out of this place. She would apologize to Dalton for not believing him completely and, more importantly, she would call the cops. *They* could deal with whatever was going on here.

She had almost reached the top of the stairs when the humming she heard grew exponentially louder. It was now more than the sound of herself and a child humming a lullaby in unison. It was the sound of an entire choir humming. More accurately, an entire *children's* choir.

Esther rounded the final section of the spiral staircase and entered the top of the treehouse tower. From within the small enclosure, she looked across the wooden bridge. The boy was no longer alone. The bridge was jam-packed with children of all shapes, colors, and sizes. The tower on the other side of the bridge was brimming with children as well. Red, brown, yellow, black, and white. They were all smiling, and humming the lullaby.

"Esther!" Abby yelled from below. "Esther! Are you seeing this?"

"I see it," she yelled back. "What should I do?"

If Abby answered, Esther didn't hear it. The volume of the hummed tune rose, and continued to rise, until it became almost deafening. The tower in which Esther stood vibrated along to the lullaby. Esther counted at least twenty-five children smiling at her.

As she took a single step back toward the spiral staircase, the little black boy rushed her. His companions followed him. The boy thudded straight into her chest. His hands clawed at her body like the velociraptor on his shirt would have if it were real. His fingernails dug deep into the exposed flesh of her left arm where she had ripped her shirt sleeve off. Scratch marks covered her arm and left red lines that vandalized her tattoos.

The force of him slamming into her chest caused her to fall backwards. She tumbled head over heels all the way back down the spiral staircase. The back of her head slammed onto the floor. It hurt, but not as much as it would have if the floor hadn't been padded.

The breath was knocked out of her. She looked up. The room was spinning, but she could see the boy standing at the bottom of the stairs. His friends stood just behind him. More children poured out of every nook and cranny the playground had to offer. They walked toward Esther with big grins and wide eyes on their tiny, no longer innocent-looking faces.

Esther rose up onto her elbows and crawled back a bit.

"We can help you!" she yelled. "All of you. We will get you out of here. Trust us. We're adults!"

The little black boy jerked his head sideways, as if cracking his neck. He stared straight into Esther's eyes.

"Get out?" he said in a puzzled tone. His voice was soft and high. "Get out?"

"Yes," Esther said reassuringly. "We're leaving this awful place. Come with us."

The boy jerked his head again. "No," he said. "We don't want to leave."

"But why?" she asked, genuinely dumbfounded.

The boy crouched a bit. He appeared to be getting ready to pounce once again.

"It's dangerous out there in the world," he said. "I'm never leaving the church."

"But why should—"

He interrupted her. "You and your friend shouldn't leave either. You're here now. Out there is the Devil's playground. Everyone out there is gonna burn in Hell. My momma told me we're safe as long as we stay in church."

"Sorry," Esther said, "but we're leaving." She got to her feet.

The boy pointed at her. "SAVE THEM!" he yelled at the top of his lungs.

The crowd of children repeated his words, shouting "SAVE THEM!" in unison.

"Let's save them!" the boy cried out as he lunged at Esther for a second time. She barely moved out of the way in time. She turned to run and slammed into Abby.

"This way!" Abby shouted as she changed direction and ran. Esther followed her.

The children gave chase. They chanted, "SAVE THEM! SAVE THEM! SAVE THEM!" as they ran.

"Where's the exit?" Esther asked as she ran after Abby.

"Just through there," Abby said, pointing at a pair of double doors. A sign above them read in bold letters, *KING'S KIDS CHILDREN'S CHURCH.* The two women sped toward the doors. Just before they reached them, the doors burst open. Children came pouring out like a horde of little zombies.

"SAVE THEM! SAVE THEM! SAVE THEM!"

Esther and Abby screeched to a halt.

"Back this way!" Abby shouted, grabbing onto Esther's hand. The women turned and ran back through the playground equipment.

"We're surrounded!" Esther shouted. She spun around, looking for an exit. There was none. All she saw was a sea of approaching children.

"Shit!" Abby yelled.

Esther turned to see that a little girl had latched onto Abby's leg. She was biting hard through Abby's jeans and tearing into her calf.

"Ouch! What the…" Esther yelled. She looked down and saw that she now had a kid of her own biting down onto her leg. She kicked her leg hard, trying to fling the child off. It didn't work. The kid only bit down harder. "Fuck!" Esther screamed. She usually tried to not curse in front of kids, but these were extenuating circumstances. She reached down and ripped the child off her as if she was ripping off a leech. A large chunk of her pants and her leg came with it. The kid chewed at the flesh as if it was a wad of bubblegum. A tiny piece of fabric from Esther's pants hung from the child's bottom lip. She shoved the kid away just as another set of teeth clamped down onto her other leg. She looked down and saw a little boy's face staring up at her. He dug his fingernails into her thigh muscles. She punched the child right in the nose.

"I just punched a kid!" Esther yelled to Abby. She looked over and saw that Abby was having a harder time than she was. She was covered with kids that swarmed like a school of piranhas.

"I've punched five," Abby yelled back. She ripped a biting child off herself and threw her away from her. The tiny body flew over the heads of the other kids and crashed into others as if they were bowling pins.

Abby kicked a girl in the stomach. "I don't want to kill a kid, Esther. But I'm afraid they're gonna kill us if we don't do something fast."

Esther looked around while using the palm of her hand to push a boy's forehead away. She saw nowhere to run. She looked up and noticed that they were standing under the monkey bars.

"Up!" she shouted. She flung the boy off of herself and then jumped up to grab onto the bars. She tried pulling herself up, but she was too heavy. A kid clung to each of her ankles. She kicked violently and, thankfully, they fell off. She pulled herself up through the bars until she was perched on top of the monkey bars like a gargoyle. Abby was holding onto the bars, but she was slipping. A group of children were holding onto her legs and tugging.

"Help!" she cried.

Esther grabbed Abby's hands and used every bit of strength she had to hoist her up. One of the kids that must have had the best grip of the lot came up with her. Esther used her injured foot to kick the boy off the monkey bars. He landed on the heads of his friends.

"What do we do now?" Esther asked.

The crowd of children had their arms raised above their heads, reaching for them. They continued to chant, "SAVE THEM! SAVE THEM!"

"I have an idea." Abby said. "We can't make it to the exit. But I know of a kind of secret passage." She pulled a ring of keys from her pocket. "It's in that janitor's closet over there." She pointed at a closet door on the other side of the playground. "If you can make a distraction, maybe you can buy me enough time to unlock that door. Then you can run to it."

Esther nodded her understanding.

"Whenever you're ready," Abby said.

Carefully, Esther stood up on top of the monkey bars. "Get ready," she told Abby. She cupped her hands around her mouth and shouted down at the children. "Hey! I don't like this church. I've been hurt too much. I'm gonna leave this place and never come back!"

At this, the children quieted. It was as if her words had shocked them into a stunned silence. Esther squatted, then used all her strength to jump off the monkey bars. Her body ached. She landed with a crash into the side of one of the treehouses. She crawled into it through a window-like opening and then turned to look at the children.

"Catch me if you can!" she yelled.

The children looked at each other and then back at Esther.

"SAVE HER!"

As Esther had hoped, they all came charging after her. She waited until they were close, then took off running across the nearest wooden bridge. Out of the corner of her eye, she saw Abby sneakily climb down from the monkey bars and start in the direction of the janitor's closet. The kids started to cross the bridge. When the leader of the pack got close enough to Esther that he was almost within biting distance, she dropped onto one of the slides.

"You can't catch me!"

It had been ages since she had slid down a slide. In a way, she still *wasn't* sliding down a slide. It was spiral and covered, like a water slide without the water. She could have used some water to help her get moving. Instead of sliding, it was more like she was sitting on her butt and crawling forward. Her hands and feet made loud squealing noises as she pushed and pulled at the plastic surface, trying to force herself down faster. Her body twisted. She was too tall, and the curves of the slide were too close together. It was hot and dark inside the tunnel, and it seemed as if she would never get to the bottom.

Just when she saw the literal light at the end of the tunnel, she heard the noise of children coming down the slide behind her. Her bare feet hit the padded floor of the playground and she stood. Before she had a chance to run, a boy rocketed out of the bottom of the slide and slammed into the back of her legs. Her knees buckled and then slammed onto the floor. She tried to stand but a girl was on her back. She threw the girl off but another girl replaced the one she had just gotten rid of. That girl was joined by another child, and then another, until so many kids were on her that she fell to the floor face first. She felt like a football player that had been tackled, the other team continuing to pile on. The weight of the kids on top of her pressed her to the floor. It was as if the floor were sucking her into itself. She put the palms of her hands on it and pushed up. It was no use—between the squishiness of the ground and the weight of the children, she was trapped. To make matters worse, the kids starting biting and scratching again.

I'm literally going to be eaten alive.

Her head jerked back as a patch of her hair was ripped out. Someone bit into her neck like a vampire. Tiny baby teeth chomped down onto every part of her. She went limp. She thought about how she and Dalton had come to a decision that they would never have kids. She had been rethinking that decision recently, but hadn't spoken with him about it. It no longer mattered. And funnily enough, it would be kids that would kill her. Her last thoughts would be of Dalton and how she wished she could see him one more time. She closed her eyes and accepted her fate.

"Get off her!" a voice roared.

The sound pulled Esther back from the brink. Her eyes opened. The massive weight on her back lessened. Someone was helping her. She growled and somehow was able to roll onto her back. She started to fight again, punching and kicking. Her elbows buried themselves into kids' faces. There was now only one boy on top of her. He was lifted off and thrown like a bag of trash being tossed into a dumpster.

Esther took in a deep breath. A man stood above her with his hand offered to her.

"Need a lift?" he said. Kids continued to attack him, but he used his free hand to push them away.

"Dalton!" Esther exclaimed. Her eyes filled with tears. She reached out and took his hand, and he pulled her to her feet. She wanted to hug him and never let go, but this was not the time. Tiny hands had already started grabbing at her again.

"Over here!" a voice cried out.

Esther turned to see Abby standing next to an open door.

"Hurry!" Abby yelled.

Esther pushed a girl over and ran, pulling Dalton along with her. She lowered her shoulder and ran straight through a few more kids on her way to the janitor's closet. She could hear the sound of the rest of the children's small feet slapping against the padded floor as they gave chase. Once again, her life depended on outrunning a pack of pursuing animals.

She leapt over a seesaw, knowing that Dalton would follow her lead. Even as she sprinted into the closet, she didn't let up, and slammed into the back wall. A mop handle smashed into her forehead and her shin hit against a yellow mop bucket. Dalton threw his hands up, trying to stop himself from colliding with her. He was mostly successful. His chest bumped into her and caused her head to ram into the mop handle again. They turned in unison and watched as Abby slammed the door shut, just in time to stop the throng of children from getting in.

A HOLY GHOST
SEVEN YEARS AGO

Abby sat on the edge of the new baptismal tank, soaking her feet in the cool water. It was her fourteenth birthday. Her father had joked that the new tank was her gift. She was only slightly worried that he hadn't been joking.

"Happy birthday to me," she said aloud. She kicked one foot up out of the pool as hard as she could. Droplets of water danced through the air and then rained down on her head. She repeated the action with her other foot. She imagined she could see each individual droplet of liquid as it flew. The water almost appeared to be glowing. This was most likely because of the stage lighting that was pointed directly at her, or more accurately at the stage in which the baptismal was installed.

The tank more resembled a swimming pool than any baptismal tank she had ever seen. It was genuinely cool, like something a millionaire would install in their mansion. Her dad had a remote control that could open up a portion of the stage to reveal the pool at the push of a button.

"We can just about baptize the whole congregation at once in this baby!" her dad had joked. Once again, she *assumed* it was a joke. She actually did wonder just how many congregants could fit into the pool at once.

With both feet once again soaking in the water, Abby lay back, resting her head against the surface of the stage and covering her eyes with her forearm.

"I miss you, Mom," she whispered.

Her mom *obviously* wouldn't be attending whatever birthday festivities her father had planned—if he had any planned at all, because she was dead.

Fuck cancer, Abby thought. Then she immediately said a quick prayer of repentance for thinking a dirty word.

Tears rolled down her cheeks. Because of the way she was lying on the floor, one droplet went into her ear.

Stop being such a baby, she told herself.

"You're the woman of the house now," she said aloud. "Time to start acting like it."

It wasn't that her dad was a bad father, but ever since Abby's mom had died, he had thrown himself into church work to take his mind off of his grief. One of the deacons had told him that it was his fault she had died, because he hadn't believed enough for her to be healed. He hadn't been the same since.

Is it my fault, too? Abby wondered. *Did I not pray enough?*

Other than how much time the church took away from him, her dad was actually great. It was just that things were happening in her life that could only be described as *girl issues*, and her father wasn't very approachable about such subjects. Lately, he only wanted to talk about how Abby was doing *spiritually*. She didn't mind talking about that. She did love Jesus. But something her dad had talked to her about recently had really gotten under her skin.

Her teacher had made her write a paper on what kind of career she wanted when she was older. She had written that she wanted to take over her daddy's church one day, as lead pastor. She had explained to her teacher that she felt *called by God* to do so. She was now fairly certain that her teacher was an atheist, or a Satanist, or something. She had failed the assignment, and her paper had been littered with red marks. At first this had bothered her, but then she remembered: *blessed are those who are persecuted because of righteousness.*

Despite the failing grade, she had been excited for her father to read the paper. She knew that he would be proud of her for the stand she had taken for Christ. To her surprise, after reading it he had shaken his head.

"I'm sorry, honey," he had told her, sitting behind his office desk. "I don't say this to be mean, but women can't be preachers." He dropped the school assignment into the rubbish bin beside his desk.

All those old papers on your desk, she remembered thinking, *and the one you throw away is mine?*

"You can be on the worship team," he continued. "You can serve in so many other ways. But the Bible is clear on this subject. It says so in 1 Timothy. Hillside is a Bible-believing church, so we believe it."

Why am I thinking about this? she wondered. *And how much longer is he going to be?*

She was sick of waiting. She always seemed to be waiting on him, whenever they had to "Just run by the church for a second."

She wiped tears from her face.

"Pastors are always running late," an unfamiliar voice said, "aren't they?"

Abby sat up so fast she almost fell head first into the baptismal tank. Her abdominal muscles burned.

A man she had never seen before approached her. He looked old, but not in physical terms, not exactly. It was more like he belonged to a different time. He wore pleated dress pants and a button up shirt tucked securely into his slacks. A braided brown belt wrapped around his waist. As he stepped up next to her, she noticed that his shoes matched his belt. They had no laces and a copper penny had been shoved into a little slot on the tongue area of each shoe.

"Mind if I join you?"

She knew she should say no. She knew she should run to her daddy's office and let him know that a stranger was somewhere they weren't supposed to be. But there was something about this man. He had a way about him. He seemed...

"You shouldn't be here," Abby told him. "My dad owns this church."

The man stepped out of his shoes. His bare feet were close enough to her that she could see the tiny hairs on his toes.

"I thought the church belonged to Jesus?" he said. He bent and began to roll up his pant legs.

"You know what I mean," Abby responded. "My dad is the pastor here. He wouldn't be okay with a stranger in the baptismal area."

The man sat at the edge of the pool and dropped his legs into the water.

"Welcome one another," he said, quoting scripture that Abby knew well.

She finished the Bible verse with him: "Therefore, just as Christ has welcomed you, for the glory of God."

Abby squinted at the man suspiciously.

"Does that verse exclude strangers?" he asked.

"Quite the opposite," she admitted. "Still, that doesn't mean a fourteen-year-old girl has to be the one to welcome you."

The man laughed. "Very true. Very wise. Go to your dad if you want to. I promise not to stop you."

Abby's facial muscles relaxed. She looked into the water at her feet and shrugged her shoulders. "Nah," she said. "He'd probably call the cops on you."

"I wouldn't want that," the man said, and laughed softly.

"So, what's your name? What's your deal?"

"My deal?" He looked up, as if the answer to her question was floating just above his head. "Honestly, I'm still trying to figure that out myself. But I figured as long as I'm here I could try to do some good."

"What good?"

"Well, for starters I was wondering why you were sitting here, on your birthday, trying to fill up this baptismal with your tears."

Abby blushed.

"It's not nice to spy on teenage girls," she said. She was starting to question her judgment, sitting here on the edge of a pool with a strange man, discussing her life.

What if he wants to hurt me?

"I wasn't spying," he said. "I just happened to be near. It was just as much a shock to me as it was to you, I promise."

Abby believed him. She didn't know why, but she did.

"I'm waiting on my dad," she told him. "I'm hoping he has something planned for my birthday tonight."

"I'm sure he does. He's your dad. He loves you."

"I never said he doesn't love me," she said defensively. "It's just, he doesn't always allow himself to show it. And... he gets real busy. The church requires a lot of attention."

"I know the type. But Abby, why were you crying? Surely you were thinking of something more than what your dad may or may not have planned?"

Abby looked back down at the water.

"To be honest, I was thinking about my future."

"Futures are sometimes tricky things to think about," the man said. He lifted one hairy foot out of the water and looked at it. It was as if he were examining it, like he couldn't believe it was there.

"Yeah," Abby said as she studied his unusual behavior. "Tricky things. Anyways... I was mostly thinking about how stupid it was of me to think that God had called *me* to be a pastor at this church one day."

The man stopped examining his foot and returned his full attention to Abby.

"What?" he asked. "Why would you think you're stupid for believing such a thing?"

"Because," Abby answered, "women can't be preachers. The Bible says so."

"The Bible says a lot of things, Abby. But it rarely says the things we *say* it says."

"Huh?" Abby said.

"Do you know the bit of scripture that states, 'No weapon that is formed against thee shall prosper'?"

"Isaiah 54:17," Abby said quickly, as if she was trying to win a contest.

"Impressive," the man said through a wide grin. "Somebody's been studying for Bible quiz." He scooted a tad closer to her. "Have you ever noticed how some people like to weaponize scripture?"

Abby nodded her head—yes, she had noticed that—but she lowered her eyes in shame at the same time. It seemed disrespectful to talk about the holy scriptures in such a way.

"Abby, look at me," the man said. "Please."

Abby looked up. Her eyes were once again wet with tears. They fell down her cheeks and mixed with the waters of death and resurrection.

"No weapon shall prosper. Not even when the weapon is a Bible being held like a gun to your head. There is love in your heart. That love is God's love, and God is love. Don't let a man with a loaded Bible take that away from you."

Abby's body shook. It felt like her bones had frozen and then thawed in an instant.

Be healed in the name of Jesus.

She collapsed. Her body tumbled face first into the water. The liquid took her into itself. She imagined herself a baby in a womb. Somehow, the man was right there. He pulled her out of the water and held her head above the surface. She embraced him, not caring one bit that she didn't know him. His kindness had shaken her to the core. Freedom that before now she had only claimed to know had become undeniably real.

"Thank you," she told the man as they embraced. He smelled funny, but good, like Jolly Ranchers. "Thank you so much."

"Anytime," he told her. "It feels good to be helpful again."

After they separated, there was an awkward moment of silence.

"I'm sorry," Abby said suddenly. "I never got your name."

The man smiled. "My name is Marvin Stone," he told her, "but most people call me Uncle Marvin."

"Abby?"

Abby jumped and turned in surprise. She had spun so quickly that her wet hair had thrown droplets of water through the air that had rained back down into the pool. Small waves moved toward the edge of the baptismal tank.

Her father stood at the opposite end.

"Who were you talking to, honey?" Pastor Teddy asked.

Abby touched her head and clenched her jaw. She was definitely in trouble. She knew that her father would be angry that she was in the pool to begin with. Add to that the fact that she was in the pool with a strange man. He would be livid. He had every right to be, and she didn't have the first clue how to explain what was going on.

"Sorry, Daddy," she said sheepishly. Water dripped from her chin. She pushed her red hair out of her face. "I was just talking to…"

She spun around to introduce her dad to this Uncle Marvin who had been so kind to her. To her astonishment, no one was there. She turned back to face her father.

"Jesus. I was talking to Jesus, Daddy."

Pastor Teddy smiled a big smile.

"That's my girl," he said. He offered her his hand and she took it. "Now, are you ready to go celebrate your birthday?"

Abby grinned up at him. "I sure am."

Her dad's strong arm pulled her up out of the water, as if she was still a little girl. Her feet landed gently on the stage. The air that was usually cold within the church was now freezing against her wet skin. Her teeth chattered.

Before she knew it, she was warm within her father's embrace.

"I'm getting you wet, Dad!"

"I don't care," he said. "I'll be your towel."

"If you say so." She rubbed her face exaggeratedly against his polo shirt.

"Come on!" he said through his laughter. He picked her up and threw her over his shoulder, then started walking away from the baptistery.

"My shoes!" Abby shouted. She reached back toward where they sat beside the pool of water.

"Leave 'em," Pastor Teddy said. He didn't stop walking. "We'll get you some new ones."

"What do you have planned, Dad?"

"It's a surprise."

"Dad!"

"Okay, okay," he said in a playful tone of defeat. "You wanna go thrift-store shopping? I'll buy you as many old T-shirts as you want."

A joyful heart is good medicine.

"Sounds perfect," she said, and she meant it.

As her father carried her off the stage and away from the inexplicable encounter she had just had, she decided to write the experience off as a necessary imagined intervention. Whether it had actually happened or not wasn't as important as how she now felt, within her soul. She was a new creation. She was a beloved daughter, with whom God was well pleased.

WINGS LIKE EAGLES

The dark, cramped quarters of the maintenance closet made Dalton borderline claustrophobic. The sound of children's fists slamming against the closed door didn't help. The noise was like a hailstorm.

Behold, they stand at the door and knock.

A light clicked on. It was dim, providing enough light to see, but not enough to chase every shadow away. The young redheaded girl that had ushered him and Esther into the salvation of a mop closet must have flipped a light switch. With his vision restored, Dalton now noticed how injured Esther was. She was crumpled on the floor. Her clothes were ripped and torn. Bite marks covered her dark skin. A small tooth was stuck inside one of the bitten areas on her forearm where a chunk of her flesh was missing.

"Are you okay?" Dalton asked, falling to his knees beside her. His hands danced around her but didn't actually touch her. He couldn't decide where to apply pressure first.

"Not really," she said through a grimace. She held out her left arm. "One of those bastards bit off my favorite tattoo."

Dalton knew exactly which tattoo she meant. Her dove was missing. He used his index finger and thumb to pull the tooth gently out of the open wound, where the tattooed dove had once perched on her skin. A string of saliva mixed with blood clung to it.

"We need to bandage her up," he said. He looked up at the other woman. "What's your name?"

"I'm Abby."

"Abby, is there a first aid kit in this closet?"

Abby didn't answer, but she immediately started digging through the supplies in the closet. Dalton turned his attention back to Esther.

"I'm so sorry for getting you involved in this."

"No," Esther told him. She grabbed weakly at his shirt. "Don't be sorry. *I'm* sorry. I'm sorry for not believing you, and for saying I believed you when I had doubts."

Dalton smiled. He wanted nothing more than to pull her into a tight embrace. He wouldn't, though. Hugging her would just cause her more pain.

He settled for using the bottom of his shirt to apply pressure to a bleeding spot on the back of her hand.

"A little doubt is the most natural thing in the world," he said. "We both know that. Doesn't mean we don't believe."

He winked at her. She squeezed both of her eyes shut and then slowly opened them. Blood tried its best to hold her eyelids together. It was caked in her eyelashes.

"No luck with a first aid kit," Abby said, dropping to her knees beside Dalton. "But I did find this." She held out a large roll of duct tape. "Could this work?"

Dalton noticed Esther's recoil slightly.

All these years, and yet the trauma still remains.

Goosebumps appeared on her skin in the few areas that weren't bitten or scratched. Her teeth began to chatter and her body shivered.

"I forgot how cold it is in this church," she said.

His heart beat harder, as if it was knocking at a door in his chest. It wanted that door flung open so it could jump out and be even closer to Esther. He knew the Sunday-school memory playing behind her bloodshot eyes. He didn't want to cause her to relive it, but her injuries were significant enough that he might have to.

"No," he said. He motioned for Abby to take the tape back. "Keep looking for a first aid kit."

"Wait," Esther interjected. "It's okay, Dalton. Use the tape." She held out her arm and looked away. "I'm ready."

Dalton sighed. Esther had always been the strongest woman he knew. This was just like her. It wasn't that she didn't get bothered by things, but she never let being bothered stop her from living life.

He wiped the blood from her injured flesh with some paper towels that Abby had found. He did his best to pinch the wounds together. Esther winced at the pain, but he could tell she was trying not to. He taped the largest of the wounds shut. While he did so, Abby worked on Esther's injured foot. She removed the blood-soaked shirt sleeve bandage and wrapped a clean rag around the foot, making sure to secure tightly the area with the missing toes.

"You've really gotten the worse of it," Abby said.

Dalton used his mouth to rip a piece of tape from the roll. "I can't believe a kid bit your toes off," he said as he wrapped the tape around the rag on Esther's foot.

"It wasn't a kid," Esther said. She tried to sit up a little better. "It was a wolf."

"A wolf?" Dalton said.

"Yeah," Abby added, "but not just any wolf. It was a pack of wolves with cracks in their skin. They had some kind of glowing lava blood inside them."

Dalton slapped his knees. "Seems about right." He looked at Esther. "I saw the witch in our car. She scared the shit out of me. It was like I was a little boy again."

Esther placed her hands on top of Dalton's.

"I ran into the church to get away," he continued. "I saw her a second time, just before I found you. She tried using the same trick on me she used when I was thirteen."

He stood and ran his hands through his long hair, then rubbed at the scar on the back of his neck. It itched.

"That's when it hit me. There's nothing new going on here. She's trying the same shit. And yeah, it's scary. But for all I know I could still be asleep in my car. Doesn't mean I'm not terrified. But I do know this: we can win."

Esther nodded in agreement. "I'm glad you're here."

"Wow," Abby said. "I can't believe it's really you. This is unreal."

Dalton turned to see her looking at him. More than looking—she was gawking. Being somewhat of a minor rockstar, he was no stranger to people staring at him. This was different, though. She spoke as if she were meeting her lifelong idol. He could tell by the Deftones shirt she wore that she was a fan of good music, but no amount of songs he had ever written could earn him the kind of look she was giving him.

"Um... are you a Starfold fan?" he asked.

"What?" Abby said in obvious confusion. "What's a starfold?"

Dalton heard Esther chuckle.

"Oh! It hurts to laugh!" she said.

Dalton rolled his eyes. He was about to awkwardly explain to Abby that he was in a pretty popular band, and that's why he had assumed she knew him, when Abby said something that made his knees weak.

"Uncle Marvin has told me all about you," she blurted out.

Bad memories always pushed to the forefront of his mind when he reflected on his time in organized religion. At the mention of Uncle Marvin, those bad memories withered. In their place, all the good memories bulldozed their way into his brain. Chief among them was the memory of Uncle Marvin saving him from punishment when he had thrown a bag of his own hair at the principal of his Christian school. The principal had floated the theory that because Dalton didn't want to follow the school's policy of no long hair on boys, he might be possessed by a demon. Dalton had cast out his demons that night by shaving his head. The next day, he had thrown that hair at his principal, who had wanted to expel him, or punch him, or maybe both. Thankfully, Uncle Marvin had been in a meeting with the principal at the time, and his cooler head had prevailed. As punishment, Dalton had been required to spend the afternoon helping Uncle Marvin rearrange and clean up puppets in the children's church. It was meant to be a punishment, but it had ended up being one of the best days he could remember.

"What did you say?" he asked in disbelief. There was no way he had heard her correctly.

"Uncle Marvin has told me all about you," she repeated.

Dalton shook his head. The closet whirled in his vision.

"That's incredible." He said as he sat down next to Esther.

"As you know, growing up a preacher's kid is difficult," Abby continued. "I've spent a lot of time alone in this church. I've... seen things."

Abruptly, Dalton's vertigo left him. He was now laser focused on this conversation.

"What kind of things?" he asked.

"Scary things. Like a witch riding on a headless deer through the sanctuary. I've seen demons of all shapes and sizes. If it wasn't for Uncle Marvin... well, he's been a big help to me over the last few years. I haven't seen him lately, though."

Dalton had no reason not to believe her. He *did* believe her. But it was when she said that Uncle Marvin had helped her that he was totally convinced.

"This is... incredible." For some reason, he held his arms open for a hug. He immediately decided that what he was doing was silly, and wondered if he was acting inappropriately. He didn't know this woman, even if she knew Uncle Marvin. Before he could drop his arms, though, Abby stepped forward and hugged him. She squeezed hard. Tears threatened to fall from Dalton's eyes. It was as if he was hugging a little sister he had never had. He didn't want to let go—but there was work to be done.

"Abby," he said as he ended the embrace. He put his hands on her shoulders and looked directly into her eyes. "I have a million questions. But first things first. Esther and I originally came here because I had a feeling..."

"And you were having dreams," Esther added from the floor.

Dalton recalled the dream that had ended with him waking up with Esther's throat in his hands.

"Yes, I was also having these crazy dreams," he said. "I knew the demonic witch had returned. And I was certain that something bad was happening in this church. We thought maybe someone was hurting women congregation members. I know it sounds crazy but..."

"We were right, Dalton," Esther said. She tried to stand and, with a little help she managed it, but she was still shaking. "I saw Pastor Teddy sacrifice Brittany, the church secretary I told you about after my interview. Pastor Teddy stuck a knife right into her chest."

Relief washed over Dalton at the news, though it was immediately chased away. He had been on the right track. He wasn't crazy, and that was a relief. But this news meant that women had died at the hands of men who proclaimed to be doing God's work. It wasn't the first time. Even so, if Dalton had anything to do with it, it would be the last time it happened on this property.

"My dad didn't do this!" Abby said defiantly.

Dalton crossed his arms and allowed her a chance to explain. He didn't mean to be defensive, but right or wrong, he had a disposition that leaned toward believing the worst about clergy.

"My dad is dead," Abby explained while looking at her feet. "I've already told Esther that my dad was murdered last year."

"Oh my God," Dalton said. "I'm so sorry to hear that."

"I'm sorry, too, Abby," Esther said. "What I meant to say was, we saw *something* that looked like Pastor Teddy killing Brittany."

Dalton said nothing, deep in thought.

Abby continued, "My dad had a good heart, but since my mom died it seemed like he cared less about people and more about preserving the culture of this church. His staff and the church board didn't help. They had very strong views that dominated their decision making."

She began to pace in the very small space available to her. "I prayed for him. I prayed that his heart would soften, but it only seemed to harden more over the years, toward everyone but me."

She looked up.

"Not that long ago, I came out to my dad." She turned and started fiddling with the corner of a big brown box full of paper towels. "He didn't handle it well at first. But then he did. Not perfectly, but I could tell his heart was changing. He told me he wanted to start moving the church in a new direction. He said I didn't have to step down from the worship team. And he even told me my girlfriend was welcome at church."

She looked back and forth between Dalton and Esther as if waiting for a response. "That's a big deal for an Alabama preacher!" she exclaimed.

"We know," they both responded.

"The staff members and church leaders didn't like it. They asked for his resignation. There was this big meeting to decide his fate. I was sitting in the reception area outside my dad's office, just looking at the fish tank. While the vote was happening, my dad came out and sat with me. He told me that no matter if he stayed as pastor or not, he would always love me."

Tears poured from Abby's eyes. She yanked a paper towel from the roll and used it to pat at her face.

"He went back into the meeting. I heard gunshots. He never came out again. Not alive, at least."

Dalton's heart became a boulder in his chest.

"I still have keys to this place," Abby continued. "I've been sneaking into the church since it happened. I left my girlfriend. I lost my job. I sleep here most nights."

"Don't the people that run this place now ever see you?" Esther asked.

"What?" Abby said. "I don't understand half the stuff you say, Esther."

"I mean, who's the pastor now?"

Abby laughed bitterly. "There is no pastor now. This place has been shut down for over a year! It's abandoned."

While Abby had been talking, Esther had been chewing at her knuckles. Now she moved her hands to her head, and her fingers disappeared into her hair. "No way!" she exclaimed. "I had an interview with somebody!"

"That's just it, Esther," Abby told her, "You didn't. I thought you were here to investigate the murders. Podcasts about shut-down churches and crazy pastors are hot right now. You wouldn't have been the first. But you were acting crazy. I thought maybe it was part of your gimmick."

"Are you trying to tell me..."

Dalton wrapped his arms around his partner. "Yes, Esther. We've been hallucinating. Or seeing into the spiritual realm. I can't explain it, but it's a lot like the last time." He looked at Abby. "Tell me what else happened tonight."

"Okay," Abby started, resuming her pacing, "when we confronted my dad's demon doppelgänger, he transformed into a werewolf. His staff and board members that shouldn't even be here also transformed."

"Those are the demon wolves you told me about," Dalton said matter-of-factly. "The ones that bit off Esther's toes."

"Yup," Esther said. She lifted her injured foot and pivoted it as if to show it off.

Dalton's face scrunched up as he considered something. Esther and Abby waited for him to process the thought.

"Okay," he said eventually. "We were brought here for a reason. I believe Uncle Marvin was trying to tell me something concerning this place, and the evil still residing here. You say you haven't seen Uncle Marvin lately?"

Abby shook her head.

"Then it's obvious what we have to do."

Abby and Esther looked at each other and then back at Dalton.

"I'm not sure it's obvious to all of us," Esther said.

"Yeah," Abby agreed, "what *do* we have to do?"

"We fight," he said. "We beat the demons. When we do, we'll know why we were brought here."

"And how do we do that, Dalton?" Esther asked, her voice high-pitched.

"It's simple," Dalton answered. "We confront the wolf and the witch."

"But they'll kill us!"

He shook his head. "No. I don't believe they will." He placed one hand on one shoulder of each of the women. "Don't misunderstand me, they can hurt us."

"No shit," Esther joked. She presented her wounds as evidence of his statement.

Their subdued laughter filled the small area.

"I've fought this kind of battle before. I can do it again."

Esther exhaled. She put bloody hands on his and Abby's shoulders. "You *can* do it again. And this time you won't be fighting alone."

"Damn right," Abby agreed. She copied them and placed a hand on their shoulders. They pulled each other close. "I'm confused as hell, but this is my fight as much as yours."

Their foreheads touched.

"Thank you both," Dalton said. He knew he couldn't do this alone. His faith was weaker than it had once been. It had shrunk over the years as doubt had crept in. Information had challenged his beliefs. He was glad that it had, but his faith was probably no bigger than a seed at this point—though seeds carry powerful potential.

"So, where was the werewolf last time you saw it?" he asked.

"The sanctuary," Esther answered.

Still holding onto one another, the three of them turned to look at the closet door. It still sounded like a herd of zombies was trying to bust in and devour them, which wasn't far from the truth. They looked back at one another.

"I can try to fight my way through the kids and then distract them long enough for you two to get back to the hallway," Dalton said.

Abby glanced at the ceiling as if she was looking for something.

"I don't like that plan," Esther admitted.

"I'm open to other suggestions."

Abby shoved a box of paper towels away, then scooted a mop bucket and a dirty-looking vacuum cleaner over. Behind them was a metal shelving unit full of cleaning products. She climbed it and stood on the top shelf. A bottle of Windex fell from one of the shelves and opened as it hit the floor. Blue liquid poured out. Abby reached for the ceiling, felt around for a few seconds, then shouted, "Got it!"

A square panel opened up in the ceiling. Looking through it, Dalton saw a metal ladder that disappeared into darkness.

Abby looked down at him. "Preachers' kids know the church better than anyone," she said with a smirk.

She turned and climbed up through the opening.

"You guys coming, or what?"

Dalton helped Esther climb the metal shelves, making sure to hold the shelf steady. By the time Esther reached the ladder in the ceiling, she was climbing on her own. She disappeared into the ceiling of the closet, and Dalton followed close behind.

***

Esther grabbed onto the last rung of the ladder. Due to her injuries, the climb to the top had been difficult. She was doing her best not to let it show, but her foot throbbed every time she pushed off to climb higher. She wondered if that was the reason it had seemed to take so long. When she reached the top, she realized that, with or without her pain, it was an extremely high climb.

The top of the ladder connected to a metal walkway. Abby was already standing on it. She reached down to help Esther up.

"Thank you," Esther said as she took the woman's hand. She pulled herself up onto the platform. Looking down, she felt as if her forehead suddenly became a brick and the weight of it was going to pull her over the railing. She grabbed onto the guard rail as tightly as she could.

She shut her eyes for a moment.

"This is *very* high."

"It's okay." Abby said. "I used to come up here all the time. It's totally safe."

"Wow!" Dalton exclaimed as he climbed onto the platform behind Esther. "This is cool. I wish my dad's church was big enough to have catwalks, when I was a kid."

It was dark, but there was just enough light to see four narrow walkways extending across the sanctuary ceiling like tiny bridges. They all connected to each other and were secured to the roof of the church by slender poles bolted into the ceiling. Esther remembered seeing the walkways when she had looked up when she had first entered the sanctuary. They had reminded her of something she might see in an industrial complex.

"This way," Abby said, gesturing for them to follow her.

They moved in single file: Abby first, then Esther, and then Dalton. The walkway was narrow. Large light fixtures were clamped onto the railings at random spots. Extension cords and colored wires were zip tied to the railings.

"Anyone see the werewolf?" Dalton asked from the rear.

"No sign of it," Abby responded. She hung her head over the edge of the railing like she knew there was no way one could fall.

Esther stopped walking and took a moment to look below. As she did so, her grip tightened on the railing. She wasn't necessarily afraid of heights, but she didn't love them either. She saw no sign of the werewolf, or its pack. The sanctuary was vast and empty. It started to spin in her vision so she decided to stop looking down and instead focus in front of her. The walkway stretched farther than she could see.

She turned to check on Dalton. He was standing on the railing like a crazy person, reaching up, trying to touch the ceiling. He still couldn't quite touch it.

"Get down," Esther snapped.

He obeyed and hurried to catch up.

"At the end of each of these walkways is another ladder," Abby said without looking back. "They all go down to different parts of the sanctuary." She stopped and looked back. "When we get down there, the demon *will* show up. I just know it. How are we going to fight it?" She was looking past Esther, at Dalton.

Dalton didn't answer. Instead, he scratched at his temple.

"Um... Abby asks a valid question," Esther said.

"I'm thinking!" Dalton responded.

"How did you beat the witch when you were a kid?" Abby asked.

"I set myself on fire and hugged her to death."

Esther looked at Abby, who buried her face in her hands and sighed.

"That's not a plan I'm okay with." Abby said.

"I'm not saying that's what we're gonna do," Dalton said. He leaned his elbows on the railing. He looked like he was contemplating the meaning of life—or something even more serious. "But to save my brother's soul, I had to be willing to lose my life. I ran across a sanctuary of poison snakes to save him. It was that reckless love that forced me to fight. So when the witch showed up to stop me, I didn't need to have a plan, I just acted. If we go down there willingly, a way to win will present itself."

"No greater love than this," Abby said. She looked like she was fighting back tears.

"Than to lay down your life for friends," Dalton finished.

The bridge beneath their feet shook violently, as if an earthquake had hit directly under the church's foundation.

"What's happening?" Esther shouted. She wrapped her arms around the railing, which vibrated against her body. The entire walkway shook as if it was a rope bridge and not made of metal. Creaking sounds that made Esther imagine bolts loosening came from all around.

"I don't like the sound of that," Dalton shouted.

"Me neither!" Esther agreed.

"Let's get to the next ladder!" Abby shouted.

The group moved in unison toward the end of the walkway. It was difficult staying upright. Esther fell to her knees more than once. Dalton helped her up and she kept moving forward. They were more than halfway across when the violent shaking stopped abruptly.

"What the hell was that?" Esther asked.

As if in answer to her question, a shriek punched her ears. It sounded like a dinosaur, or the world's loudest bird.

"What the hell was *that*?" she asked again.

"Go. Go. Go!" Dalton yelled, pushing at Esther's back.

They all ran.

"We're almost there!" Abby said. As she turned to face them, she ran into something. Esther collided with her, and Dalton slammed into Esther like the last car in a pileup.

"What is it?" he yelled from the back.

Esther looked up. There was something blocking their way. Abby was touching it with her hand, obviously trying to decide what it was. It was large, as tall as Abby, and made of what looked like... tree branches? The whole thing was a deep brown color.

"It's a bird's nest?" Abby said. She pulled a brittle-looking dead leaf off a branch and crunched it within her palm.

"Guys," Dalton said, "I think we should go back. We can try one of the other walkways."

"Let's go!" Abby said.

They all turned and started back the way they had come. Dalton now led the way. Esther had no idea what kind of bird could build such a massive nest inside a church building, and she didn't want to find out. All she really wanted now was to get down to ground level. Whatever demons she had to face, she wanted to at least face them at a lower altitude.

The bridge shook again as if an aftershock had hit. Dalton froze.

"Guys," he said. Esther heard the fear in his voice. "Turn around! Go back. Go back!"

Esther knew she shouldn't look. She should just turn and run. Instead, she leaned over and looked past Dalton's broad shoulders. There in front of her, perched on the railing of the walkway, was a beast. Its long, bony, clawed fingers and taloned feet wrapped around the railing. One foot and one hand rested on each side of the walkway. Its hunched body was covered in scales and massive feathers. Each feather looked at least as long as one of her arms. Six yellow eyes stared right at her, and between those eyes was a pointed, black beak hanging over a mouth with four sharp fangs. Two gigantic wings protruded from the creature's back and were spread wide. The tips of the wings touched the roof of the church. Under the massive wings were two muscular arms that reminded Esther very much of the werewolf's arms. They were covered in bulging veins.

Esther recognized this creature immediately. She had never seen it before, but it looked exactly as Dalton's brother James had described it when he had told her about his spiritual battles. This was the owl-beast he had fought at a Christian summer camp, years ago when he had volunteered as a camp counselor.

Esther's wrist began to itch. She looked at it. As she suspected, three numbers that weren't there before materialized as if they had been tattooed on her long ago.

666.

She looked up and noticed that Dalton was looking at his wrist, too. The numbers must have appeared on him as well.

The beast roared. The hanging walkway shook.

"Go!" Dalton shouted. His hands fumbled with something at his waist.

What is he doing? Esther thought.

She watched as his belt flew out of the belt loops on his pants. He yanked hard and flicked his belt into the air. He looked like a rock and roll version of Indiana Jones with his whip ready to strike.

He growled and charged at the monster. It gave a deep, rumbling laugh and used its clawed hands and feet to crawl across the top rail of the walkway toward Dalton.

"Dalton!" Esther screamed.

The beast kept coming. Its wings folded back as if to be more aerodynamic. Light fixtures sparked and fell from the rails as it passed.

Dalton didn't back down. Esther heard his footfalls slam against the grated floor of the metal bridge. He raised the belt high above his head. Just as he was about to collide with the creature, he swung it at the beast's six-eyed face. It was impossible to tell if the belt even made contact. All Esther could see was the creature's scaled chest crash into Dalton. The back of Dalton's head struck the grated floor. The monster didn't stop. It passed over Dalton as if he was of no consequence.

"Esther, come on!" Abby screamed.

Esther turned and ran. Abby had already climbed to the top of the bird's nest and had her hand held out for Esther to grab. The beast shrieked behind Esther. She could feel its warm breath on her neck.

She jumped and grabbed Abby's hand. Her bad foot thudded against the bird's nest and she winced as the tip of a tree branch poked into the place where two of her toes were missing. Ignoring the pain, she pushed off the branch with her foot as Abby pulled her up. The two women crashed into one another and then tumbled down together into the nest. For a moment they just lay there, motionless, their arms and legs tangled together.

"Are you okay?" Esther asked. She tried to pull her leg out from under Abby's body. A tree branch was poking her in the back.

"No," Abby grunted. She sat up. "But we gotta keep moving."

"My leg is stuck under you," Esther said.

Abby moved over a bit. Esther's leg remained stuck. That was when she realized that her leg wasn't stuck under Abby's body—it was stuck under someone else's body.

"Oh my God!"

Esther yanked her leg, hard. The naked corpse on top of her leg shifted. Flies erupted from within the body. Intestines spilled out of a ripped-open stomach cavity. Blood and guts coated Esther's leg.

She slipped her leg the rest of the way out from under the dead body and scooted away from it. It was only then that she saw the messy blonde hair, and it dawned on her that this was Brittany.

Her elbow pressed up against something pointed. She turned to push away what she believed would be another tree branch, but instead what she saw was the exposed ribcage of yet another corpse. This body had decayed far beyond Brittany's. It looked almost like a skeleton with a wig on. The bones had been chewed on and broken off in various places. What skin remained reminded Esther of dried meat. Bugs crawled in and out of every crevice. She hastily moved away from the cadaver only to accidentally crawl on top of another skeleton.

"It's the women," Abby said. She was covering her nose. "We've found the women."

The smell was putrid, like old, wet trash. It smelled like someone had thrown out an old rotisserie chicken mixed with rotting fruit. Esther choked down vomit that was trying to make its way up her throat. It tasted acidic.

Abby leaned over and puked. The vomit was the same shade of brown as the bird's nest. Flies went directly for it. At the sight of Abby's vomit, Esther's own made a resurgence. She leaned forward and spewed chunks into the mouth and eyes holes of a skull that had been picked clean of its flesh.

"How many women?" Esther asked as she wiped vomit from her chin.

Abby looked around.

"Six?" she answered. "Maybe seven? It's hard to tell."

A noise came from the edge of the nest. Esther and Abby jumped up, ready to run, or fight, or do whatever needed to be done. Dalton crawled over the edge of the nest. His nose was bloody. It looked like it might be broken. There was a dark, bloodstained patch on the front of his shirt.

Esther hobbled over to him. "Are you okay?" she asked.

Dalton held her close.

"I'm fine," he said. "But..." he rubbed the back of his head, "remind me to tell James that the whole *belt of truth* thing in his story didn't work this time." He sniffed the air a few times. "What's that smell?"

Esther didn't need to answer. Dalton shoved past her and knelt in the middle of the nest. The decaying remains of the women surrounded him. Flies swarmed him. He screamed in anger and punched at the floor of the nest until his knuckles bled.

"You can't win," a deep, monotone voice said.

Esther spun to see the owl-beast perched on the side of the nest. Despite its massive size, she hadn't heard it approach.

It laughed slowly and steadily, then continued, "I am part of a chain that cannot be broken. This chain stretches back to the foundations of reality and Hell itself. My master holds the first link securely in his grasp." The beast looked into Dalton's eyes. "And do you want to take a guess what the final link is attached to?"

Esther studied Dalton's face. It was contorted with rage.

"My family," Dalton growled.

The beast nodded its head. "Very good. Lucky the people that built this church bulldozed your family's little cemetery. Your granddaddy's bones, and his daddy's bones, and so on, are soaking in the dirt under this place. We will always live here rent-free because of it."

"We will defeat you," Abby stated.

The demon twisted its neck to look at Abby. Its six eyes blinked in unison.

"Who?" it said. "Who? Whooo! Whooo! Who are you?"

"Stop it!" Abby screamed.

The beast laughed. It leaned over the nest to get so close to Abby that its black beak almost touched her face.

It whispered, "You miss your daddy?" Then it spread its wings wide. "I'll take you to him."

The beast's wings flapped. Esther covered her face as wind buffeted her and she almost fell over backwards. Twigs and bones flew into her shins. She peeked through her fingers and saw two enormous talons wrap around Abby's petite frame. She was lifted into the air as the creature leapt across the nest and dove below the walkway, toward the sanctuary and out of sight.

Esther and Dalton scrambled to look over the edge of the nest to watch the beast gliding across the room. Gracefully, it turned back toward them, flapped its wings a few times, and then landed on the railing of the next walkway over, directly above the stage. The massive curtain blocked Esther's view of the stage itself, but she knew that if Abby was dropped from such a height she would surely die, in approximately the same area as Brittany had earlier. Abby was now held loosely within the long, bony fingers of one of the beast's muscular arms. It held her away from its body as if it was disgusted by her.

The demon looked over at Dalton and Esther and said, "It's sad... how Abby has *fallen* away."

Its fingers spread, letting go of Abby. She let out a scream. Esther watched as her friend fell to her death.

LEVIATHAN

The flight around the sanctuary had been chaotic. The blood within Abby's body rushed to her head as the demon grabbed her by the ankle. Looking up meant looking down at the stage.

The beast said something. The chaos in her mind made it difficult to understand the words. Her ankle throbbed. The monster's grip was as strong as a bear trap.

Is there anywhere safe to land?

All she could see below was the stage floor and band equipment. There was a drum cage with a soft looking fabric over it, but she was certain she would tear through the fabric and crash into the drum kit. She imagined a cymbal decapitating her. She was about to turn her attention back to the beast when something caught her eye. It was a man, waving at her from one of the other walkways.

Uncle Marvin?

"...how Abby has *fallen* away."

She was falling. Uncle Marvin vanished. As she fell, she let out a scream. Her relatively short life flashed before her eyes. She remembered her mom and wondered how she would have handled her coming out. She thought about Libby and wondered if she would take her back. She thought about her dad and her fourteenth birthday when he had taken her thrift-store shopping. That was a good day. It was also the day she had met Uncle Marvin for the first time, in the baptistery.

The baptistery!

Her fingers dived into her pocket.

Please be there!

Elation jolted through her body as her hand closed around the small remote control on her dad's spare set of church keys, which controlled the opening and closing function for the baptismal tank. She used her thumb to press a button on the remote. She wasn't positive she had hit the correct button to open the floor to reveal the pool underneath, but at the rate she was falling she only had time to guess and say a prayer. To her relief, she saw the part of the stage directly underneath her start to split open.

This is going to be close!

The floor was only a few yards away, and the baptistery had only opened about a foot wide. It was still opening, but at an excruciatingly slow rate. At least the water was now visible. Abby closed her eyes and pulled her knees in as if she was doing a cannonball at a pool party. She would either make it or she wouldn't.

Pain nipped at her knee. It wasn't bad at all. It was only like a skinned knee one might get after falling off a bike. The pain was immediately washed away by the sensation of her entire body being submerged in water. She had made it into the baptistery waters, but only barely. Her butt hit hard against the bottom of the pool. Her howl of pain was muffled, and bubbles flew from her mouth and swirled around her. She pushed off the floor and followed the bubbles up to the surface. When her head breached the water she took in a deep breath of cold air. She watched as the opening floor panels finished opening the rest of the way. She had been baptized before, when she was a kid. She had often thought that maybe she should be baptized again as an adult, now that she understood the meaning behind it more clearly.

"This counts," she told herself.

She looked up, searching for the beast. It was nowhere to be seen. Then she looked at the walkways for any sign of Dalton or Esther, but the closed stage curtain blocked her from seeing the walkway.

She waded over to the side of the pool. She had to get back to Esther and Dalton. They only stood a chance if they were together.

She was halfway out of the pool when something grabbed her from behind and pulled her back in. Her head submerged so fast she wasn't even able to take in a breath. Whatever had a hold of her was strong. Its arms were wrapped around her. She kicked and tried to hit it with her elbows, but it wouldn't let go. She craned her neck to the point she was afraid it would snap. She needed to see what was trying to kill her. What was *going* to kill her. As if it knew what she was thinking, her attacker spun her around and let her go.

With her eyes open under the water, she saw something confusing. It wasn't at all what she had been expecting. The sight made her forget that she was in desperate need of air.

It was her father. His bald head, face, and beard looked exactly like they should, but his eyes were glowing red. Two antlers poked out from the top of his head, their pointed tips sticking out above the surface. He also had wings. They were the wings of the beast that had dropped her. Long brown feathers swished back and forth in the water. The wings reached all the way to each side of the pool. Her father's legs looked different as well. They were more muscular, and they were covered with fur. His feet were large and clawed like a... like a werewolf's.

You are not my father! her mind shrieked.

Remembering she needed to breathe, she kicked up and surfaced. Wasting no time, she grabbed the edge of the pool and climbed out. She tensed, expecting to be grabbed from behind again and pulled back in. She wasn't. Dripping wet, she backed away from the baptistery, but didn't take her eyes off it. The water within the tank began to bubble. It boiled. Steam rose from the surface of the water as if someone had turned on one of the church's smoke machines.

"What now?"

Something poked out of the surface of the boiling water. It resembled the beak of a dolphin. It was soon joined by two more blue-green *things*. They grew at a rapid pace. All three of them shot high up into the air. They now looked like the necks of brontosauruses, without heads. A wave of water breached the baptismal tank and washed over Abby's feet. She turned and watched it flood under the stage curtain. She could hear it pour over the edge of the stage like a waterfall and splash onto the sanctuary floor.

When she turned around again, the three stalks sticking out of the baptismal were bent over, close together, and looking right at her with black eyes from which oozed equally black liquid. It looked like they were crying tar. The stalks had each grown a long, pointed horn. The area under the horns split open, revealing multiple rows of sharp teeth. Abby could see at least five rows.

Two appendages burst out of the pool and slammed onto the stage on either side of Abby. They looked like legs that a dragon from a fairy tale might have. Each was as large as a tree trunk and covered with shiny scales. The floor beneath her trembled. Three claws on each appendage dug deep into the wood of the stage, scratching and throwing splinters into the air.

"What in the book of *Revelations* is that?"

All three of the monster's heads roared. Abby saw even deeper rows of teeth that she hadn't noticed previously. The monster's body lifted farther out of the baptismal tank. She could now see its chest. In its center was what she assumed was another mouth, or maybe a forward-facing rectum? Whatever it was, the massive, black, pulsating hole, with a bit of wrinkly pink inside, was big enough to swallow her. It expanded, and the same black liquid that had leaked from the creature's eyes exploded from it like projectile vomit or diarrhea, splashing Abby's face and body. The force of the impact was so strong that she fell onto her backside and slid into the stage curtains.

She wiped at her eyes and then opened them. Thankfully, none of the sticky goo had gotten in. The floor in front of her was now completely covered with black, like freshly lain asphalt.

A third leg crashed onto the floor. Black ooze splashed into the air. The monster roared.

Abby lifted the curtain behind her and rolled under it, making her escape.

***

Esther's feet touched the floor of the sanctuary. Dalton was right behind her. The ladder had deposited them toward the back of the room. They had climbed down quickly, as if reaching Abby's body sooner rather than later would save her.

Esther ran down the center aisle, between the very chairs through which she had been chased by murderous men not long ago. She knew Abby was dead, but still she ran to save her. Far ahead of her was the stage. She wished the curtain was open so she could receive the closure she desired. Its fabric hung heavy like a death shroud.

Dalton, being injured but not near to the level that Esther had been, sprinted past her, as if the same thoughts of reaching Abby faster as a means of resurrection dominated his mind as well.

"Hurry!" he shouted needlessly.

Esther could do nothing less. She was halfway to the stage, Dalton a bit closer, when something unexpected happened. Water spurted out from underneath the curtain and poured over the edge of the high stage. It splashed onto the sanctuary floor and spread out, creating puddles that went beyond the first rows of chairs.

Dalton and Esther stopped running.

"What now?" she asked.

Dalton grabbed her hand.

"Esther," he said, "whatever comes out from behind that curtain, we fight it together."

Even though it caused her pain, she squeezed his hand tightly.

"I'm with you."

A monstrous roar sounded out. The noise was so stupendous that it was impossible to determine from which direction it came. It was all-encompassing, as if the entire sanctuary was one big speaker blasting out the sound in every direction. The only clue as to the origin of the roar was the fact that the thick stage curtain shook as if a heavy wind had blasted it from the other side.

Esther's entire body tensed. Dalton squeezed her hand.

"We fight whatever comes from behind the curtain?" she asked, her voice trembling.

She imagined the curtain falling in majestic fashion to reveal a beautiful yet terrifying T-Rex in a classic *Jurassic Park* roaring pose. Instead, out from under the curtain rolled a small figure, which fell off the stage and hit the ground running. It took a second for Esther to even recognize the figure as human. It was covered from head to toe in a black, gooey substance. Two white eyes looked out from within the black.

"Go!" the person yelled as they ran toward them. The voice was familiar—familiar enough to make Esther's heart leap for joy even in the midst of such terrifying circumstances.

"Abby!" she shouted. She rushed toward the woman.

"Go!" Abby shouted again. She waved them away frantically. "Go! Go! Go!"

The curtain behind Abby fell. The motion was far from majestic. The curtain didn't float toward the ground, but was pulled from whatever cords held it in place. Two long spikes, like the jousting lances of medieval knights, poked through it. It then ripped down the middle with a loud tearing sound.

A blue-green head with a large horn emerged from the rip, shooting out toward the three friends like some kind of 3D movie effect. The horn barely missed impaling Abby in the back. Two more heads exactly like the first appeared. Pieces of torn fabric from the curtain hung from their horns like capes.

"Go!" Abby screamed again.

She approached Esther and Dalton and then ran past them on her way out of the sanctuary.

"Come on!"

Two legs shot over the edge of the stage and crashed to the sanctuary floor. There was another roar, then all three heads bent low to the ground and swept from left to right and then back the opposite way. It knocked chairs out of the way. They flew through the air and slammed into the far-off walls of the church.

Esther turned to follow Abby, pulling Dalton with her.

Abby had already reached one of the corridors that led to the exit. As Esther entered the corridor, she saw Abby yanking at the doors with all her might. From behind, she looked more like herself, as there was far less black substance on her rear, revealing areas of white skin and her red hair.

"We're locked in!" Abby shouted.

Esther ran to her, pulling in vain at the locked doors.

"We have to fight it," Dalton said.

Esther whirled around. "Are you kidding me? We can't fight that!"

Abby stopped yanking on the doors, and turned. She took a deep breath and then said, "If anyone says to this mountain, 'Go, throw yourself into the sea,' and does not doubt in their heart but believes that what they say will happen, it will be done for them."

"But..." Esther said, "but I do doubt. I doubt very much. I'm so sorry, but I have all kinds of doubts that I keep to myself and just pretend aren't there."

Abby held Esther's hands. "So do I, but those doubts are in my head." She pointed at her chest. "My heart believes."

"It's the same for me," Dalton chimed in. "Sometimes, when people ask if I'm still a Christian, I want to answer, 'Depends on what day, hour, or sometimes minute, you ask me.' But my heart has been like an anchor dropped and holding me to a truth beneath the surface I know is there but I can't see. Whenever I stray, I always feel the anchor tugging at my heart."

Esther reached for Dalton's hand. "Your heart is why I love you. I know what goes on in your head is enough to drive you mad."

Dalton took her outstretched hand, breathed out a laugh, and lowered his forehead to her shoulder.

"But what's in your heart, I trust it completely," Esther said.

"We doing this, or what?" Abby asked.

They walked together, three as one, as confidently as they could back into the sanctuary. Whatever faith they needed to win was inside them. Together they would find it.

THE PREYER CHAIN

The monster had calmed. Its breathing was deep. It had switched from berserk to meditative in mere moments. It stood motionless in the center of the sanctuary on its four dragon legs like an ancient statue. What chairs remained in its vicinity were flattened. The creature's three heads were now arranged in a triangular formation, two on the bottom and one on top. Its three long necks twisted around one another like braided hair. Esther thought that in its calm state it was almost *more* terrifying.

Its inky black eyes followed her as she, Dalton and Abby approached. The only plan they had agreed upon amounted to stubborn defiance. Most concerning was the flexing black hole in the creature's chest. It was from the hole that breaths were being taken as air was inhaled and exhaled. The monster lowered itself to the ground so that it was sitting on its belly and its chest was level with them. Hot air blasted Esther in the face, along with black particles of goo. It smelled like rot. She imagined that the hole led to the belly, and the belly was like a landfill of putridity. She didn't want to go into the hole, but she was drawn to it nevertheless. Her steps had become lighter the closer she got to it, as if the floor had become a moving sidewalk. It wasn't that she couldn't fight her forward momentum—it was more like she knew the hole was her final destination. It opened wider, as if inviting the trio in.

The heart of a man plans his way, but the Lord establishes his steps.

Esther, Abby, and Dalton walked willingly into the open jaws of evil, a portal to Hell from which they knew not if they would return.

***

Esther blinked and the lights came back on. She was... somewhere else. Somewhere familiar, but also very far away.

The small room was cold and the walls were painted blue, like the ocean. Noah's Ark floated in the middle of her vision. Cartoon animals with grinning faces poked out of the big brown boat. Fish swam through her memory and morphed into drowning people.

Oh my God, she thought. *Why am I here?*

She was sitting in a metal chair. She looked down at her left arm, expecting to see the arm of the child she had once been. Instead, it was her arm, tattoos and all. Also, there were no injuries. It was as if the events of this terrible night hadn't happened—but there was still pain. The pain was only in one spot on her left arm, right where her dove tattoo was. She looked down at her feet. She was wearing Converse shoes. She wiggled her toes and could tell that they were all there.

"Esther!" someone shrieked.

She looked up to see a woman in a long dress that would most likely have covered her ankles if her big, pregnant belly hadn't claimed so much of the material. Her ankles looked swollen.

"Hope?"

"It's Mrs. Hope to you, Esther," the pregnant woman answered. "Now, if you're done letting the Devil use you to distract this class... I was wondering if you would be my volunteer?"

Esther's dove tattoo burned, as if the inked feathers had caught fire. She actually looked down to see if it had. It had not, but she imagined the pain to be similar to that of a woman accused of witchcraft, the first tongues of flame licking at her heels. She stood up so fast that her chair fell back and slammed onto the ground.

"No!" she shouted. "Stay away from me!"

Hope waddled toward her. One of her arms was buried deep within her purse, searching for something. Esther knew exactly what she was searching for.

"Let God use you," Hope said in a sing-song voice. She repeated her words and when she did, every kid in every seat stood and joined her.

"Let God use you!" They chanted the words over and over again as they approached.

"Let God use you! Let God use you!"

Esther's back pressed against the wall of the classroom. Her spine turned to ice.

"Let God use you! Let God use you!"

The mob was almost upon her. Hope yanked her hand out of her bag. Within her grasp was not the roll of tape that Esther had expected to see. In its place was a large, brown feather. Holding it by its tip, Hope raised it above her head. She then turned her face up. Esther watched in disbelief as she slid the white quill of the feather down her throat. She could see the woman's esophagus move as the feather traveled down all the way until its tip disappeared. Hope swallowed and then lowered her head so she was once again looking at Esther. The screech of an owl escaped her mouth.

"What the hell?" Esther shouted.

"What the hell?" the kids all repeated. "What the hell? What the hell?"

Hope moved until she was standing only a foot away from Esther. She lifted her dress to reveal her pregnant belly.

"A little help, kids," she said, motioning to her belly with her chin.

The kids of the Sunday school class began to rip at her stomach. Tiny hands grabbed close to her belly button and yanked flesh away. Hope laughed as blood and mucus poured out and splashed the children's faces. The kids giggled. They were enjoying themselves. They threw pieces of Hope at each other as if it was a game of dodgeball. Within seconds, Hope's belly was torn completely open. The kids all stopped playing and watched in amazement.

Within the opening was something strange. It was an off-white color. Esther couldn't tell what it was until Hope grabbed her guts and pulled them further apart to reveal an egg.

"Isn't it beautiful!" Hope exclaimed.

"Beautiful! Beautiful! Beautiful!" the kids chanted.

Thin lines spiderwebbed across the surface of the egg. A tiny black beak poked away a small portion of the shell from within.

"Here it comes!" Hope said, looking down inside herself. She reached in and helped the hatching bird by pulling away small sections of eggshell.

"Oh my God," Esther whispered. The bird within the egg was a baby version of the beast that had chased her, Dalton, and Abby on the church's raised walkways. It chirped. It was almost cute.

Hope reached inside her open abdomen and gently removed the chick. She held it out, offering it to Esther.

"I did this for you."

Without thinking, Esther reached for it. She stopped only when she noticed the numbers upon her wrist.

666.

She pulled her hands back.

"I don't want it," she said defiantly.

Hope shook the chick at her.

"It doesn't matter," she said forcefully. "I made this for you, on this day. It is yours to carry. Pay attention to it. Nurture it."

Once again, Esther's hands reached for it. This time, it was not numbers on her wrist that caused her to pause, but a tattoo upon her forearm. She studied her dove tattoo. It had long been her favorite, even though it was artistically nothing special. Still, it had covered a wound that she never wished to see again.

"Hope," Esther said, pulling back her hands, "I don't want this."

The dove tattoo spread its wings and flew from Esther's forearm. As it took off, it took her pain with it.

The dove attacked the newly hatched beast within Hope's hands. Esther's mouth was agape as everything briefly became wings, talons, and feathers. Brilliant white and deep brown swirled together. When it was over, the dove was bloody but alive, while the beast had been defeated. It had multiple holes in its chest. Its head had been removed.

The dove flew back onto Esther's arm and brought peace with it.

Hope held the dead beast within her shaking hands. It vanished, as if it had never existed. In its place was a large roll of gray tape.

The scene seemed to rewind. The blood on the children's faces traveled through the air and into Hope's innards. Her abdomen started repairing itself. New flesh grew, like the surface of a lake freezing over, until everything was exactly as it was before. Hope dropped her dress, letting it cover her bulging belly. Tears rolled down her face.

"Esther," she said. Her voice quivered. "Can you ever forgive me for what I did?"

Esther took the roll of tape from Hope's hands. She dropped it on the floor and watched as it rolled away. She reached over Hope's baby bump and hugged her.

"I thought you'd never ask," she said. Tears now rolled down her face as well. "I forgive you. Don't think about it anymore, Hope. I sincerely forgive you."

***

Abby remembered this day vividly. She was sitting at the dinner table. Her dad had bought enough KFC to feed a whole family. It was just the two of them.

"Too bad Libby couldn't make it," Teddy said. "I bought enough chicken."

He plopped some mashed potatoes onto Abby's plate.

While he poured way too much brown gravy over them, she had said, *She has studying to do. Exams are coming up.*

The gravy was still pouring.

"She has studying to do. Exams are coming up." Abby said the words as if she were reading a script she had memorized by heart.

Next, her dad would say...

"That means, *you* have exams coming up. Shouldn't you be studying, too?"

As he said the words, he reached across the table for a biscuit. His arm hit his glass of sweet tea, spilling it.

Exactly how I remember it.

The dinner went on for quite some time. Utensils clinking. Kentucky Fried Chicken being consumed. Perfectly remembered small talk. *The moment* was fast approaching. Abby's stomach ached, and not because of all the fried food. No, her stomach was in knots because this was the night.

She was sick of living a lie. She would tell him the truth.

"Dad..." she began.

"Yes, dear?" he said with a mouthful of chicken.

"Um... would you pass me another biscuit, please?"

That was attempt number one. There would be a few more similar attempts before she worked up the courage to spit it out.

What am I doing back here? Abby thought. *I know what happens. He reacts poorly on this night, but soon comes around. So why am I so afraid to tell him again?*

She took the biscuit her father was holding out.

"Thank you," she said. Then, going off script, she said, "Dad, you like Libby. Don't you?"

"Of course," he answered. He peeled the crunchy brown skin off a chicken breast and shoved it into his mouth. Grease dripped from his lips.

"I like her, too," she said.

"I should hope so," he said while chewing. "You two hang out enough."

Abby put her elbows on the table and leaned forward. This wasn't exactly how it had happened, but she wanted to get it over with.

"No, Dad. I *like* her."

Teddy stopped chewing.

"As in, she's my girlfriend."

Even though Abby knew what was coming, she felt a sense of relief.

It was both an amazing night and an awful one, she thought. *Just remember, he came around. What he's about to say, he takes it back.*

Teddy didn't move. He just stared straight ahead, with a chicken leg held up to his face.

"You okay, Dad?" she remembered saying, and then said. She had honestly thought he might be choking.

Teddy didn't respond. At least, he didn't respond verbally. His body began to shake.

This is new.

Sweat droplets appeared on his bald head. Every muscle in his body tensed.

"Dad. You're scaring me, Dad." Abby stood. "Just say something, Dad."

Where are the words? she thought.

His words had been hurtful, but they were only words. This was... she didn't know what this was.

Teddy started growling.

Oh no.

A familiar fear resurfaced within Abby. She wanted to reach for Esther's hand but knew her friend wasn't there.

Teddy let out a shriek. He dropped the chicken leg and lifted his greasy hands to his face. His fingertips split and morphed into sharp, obsidian claws. In a replay of earlier events, he used his newly formed claws to scratch his face off. It fell onto his dinner plate and food splattered across the table.

Abby wanted to run away, but where would she go? She was stuck in this decaying memory.

Where her dad's face had been a wolf snout grew rapidly, just as she had suspected it would. Grayish black hair covered it. The wet, black nose sniffed at the air. Pointed teeth were revealed, a red tongue licking at them.

"Daddy, no!" Abby shouted. "Not again."

Teddy stood. He towered over her. His body had morphed as quickly as his face. He was no longer her dad—he was the wolf. She was his prey.

"NO DAUGHTER OF MINE WILL BE A PART OF THE ALPHABET MAFIA!"

Its clawed hand grabbed onto one side of the dinner table. Abby saw the muscles under the thick hair of its arm flex, just before the table was thrown to the side to slam against the wall. A bucket of chicken bounced off the ceiling like a pool ball against a side rail. Crispy chicken legs and thighs struck the floor like small meteors and scattered around Abby's feet. The table seemed to stick to the wall for the briefest of moments before it slid down and crashed to the floor. A framed family portrait still hung in the exact spot the table had hit, but its glass was broken. Mashed potatoes and gravy dripped down the frame and covered Abby's face in the portrait, and the face of her dead mom.

"The sin of homosexuality will send you straight to Hell," the werewolf said as it stomped toward Abby. She looked around. Her back was now against the wall. She hadn't noticed before, but this dining room, while very similar to the real dining room in her father's house, had a few glaring differences. It had no windows, and no doors. She was trapped. Trapped in this room. Trapped in this moment.

The wolf's head bumped into the chandelier that would normally have hung over the dining-room table. "You'll be crispy after you die. Just like a piece of fried chicken." The wolf licked at its claws. "Just like I like it. *Finger... lickin'... good.*"

The monster lunged at Abby. Pain punched her in the chest. The back of her head slammed against the wall. The wolf turned its head to one side and opened its jaws wide. Teeth sank into her torso. They stabbed into her ribs. They sank deeper and deeper inside her as the werewolf's jaws tightened like a bear trap. She was being crushed to death. The wolf would soon be dining on her innards.

She looked at the family portrait. Food was still covering the faces of her and her mother. Her father's face was still visible.

The picture of Teddy moved. It shook its small head. It mouthed words.

Abby squinted, trying to make out what it was saying.

That's not me, it said without audible words but enunciating exaggeratedly. *I love you. I don't think you're going to burn in Hell. A father's love is too strong to let that happen.*

Abby smiled. She was being devoured by a beast and yet, joy was consuming her. Her fingers clutched at the hair above the wolf's eyes and under its lower jaw. She leaned over and buried her face in the side of its head. She puckered her lips and kissed it gently. Leaning close to its ear, she whispered, "I love you."

She said this not to the wolf, but to the dad she knew had been swallowed by it.

"And I know you love me."

***

Dalton sat behind his father's desk in his childhood church. His dad's office looked just as he remembered it. The big wooden desk was there, and so was the curved green lamp with the golden pull chain. To Dalton's left was a comfortable-looking faux-leather couch. It had cracks in the leather from years of being sat on, and jumped on, and slept on, mostly by Dalton and his brother.

Speaking of James, there was a framed photo of him on their father's desk, right next to a photo of a much younger Dalton. Dalton picked up the small frame and stared unblinking at the photo.

"Where did you go?" Dalton asked his younger self.

"I, for one, miss that little boy," a shrill voice said.

Looking back over at the couch, he saw the witch sprawled across it in all her demonic glory. Her antlers were as pointed as ever. Her hair still greasy and gray, hanging heavily like dreadlocked spiderwebs. Her glowing red eyes illuminated her face within her tattered hood. This was the clearest Dalton had ever been able to see her face. It was almost beautiful—until she smiled. Blackened teeth, full of rot, jutted out from pink gums.

She patted the couch next to her. Dust particles flew into the air.

"Some good memories you made on this couch," she said. She turned and, with her back to Dalton, started making sex motions as if she had mounted someone on the couch. Her neck twisted one hundred and eighty degrees to allow her to look at Dalton. "Some not so good memories as well, huh?"

Dalton was tempted to look away, but instead he maintained eye contact.

"Ancient history."

The witch turned and collapsed back onto the couch, sinking deep into its cushions. Dalton saw the cracks in the leather expand to reveal white fabric underneath. The witch crossed her arms in front of her, as if she was upset.

"Thirteen-year-old Dalton was way more fun," she said, looking away.

"No," Dalton responded. "Thirteen-year-old me was just way more fun for you to mess with. Dalton in his forties has gotten rid of most the indoctrination that made me that way."

The witch jumped up. Suddenly, her feet were on the couch cushion where her ass had been a second ago. Her knees pointed out in front of her. She held onto them.

"But not all the indoctrination," she said with a cackle. "Not all."

Dalton leaned back in his father's chair. It felt weird being in the witch's presence and not being afraid. It was weird, but also natural, as if this was how it was always supposed to be. He reached up and rubbed at the back of his neck. It was a habit he had had since he was thirteen years old. Since the night the witch had come into his life. A small scratch she had given him had remained there. It didn't necessarily hurt, but whenever he was stressed or upset, he would always reach for it. He had tried to forget about it. He had even grown his hair out, hoping it would cover it and keep it out of mind. It had worked, *sometimes*, but he always ended up remembering it was there.

The witch grinned at him. "I'm your family curse, Dalton. I'll always be there."

Dalton smiled.

"Turns out," he said, still rubbing the back of his neck, "that's not entirely true." He lifted his long hair up into a ponytail and spun the desk chair so that his lifelong tormentor could see the back of his neck. "Your mark is gone."

The witch hissed. Dalton spun around to look at her.

"You will always be with me," he continued. "But I've decided to use that as a way to help others who have the same mental struggles that I do. To accomplish that, I have to stop fearing you."

He paused, taking a second to look at the face that had defined personal terror for his entire life. He studied it and found it... sad. It was the face of someone who scared children to make themselves feel more important.

"I'm sorry," he told her. The sympathy in his voice surprised even himself. "But I have to move on."

Her face contorted. "What are you going to do? Write a book?" She laughed, but her laugh held no mirth.

"You know," Dalton said, interrupting her forced amusement, "that's not a bad idea."

The witch lunged from the couch. Her body flew through the air toward Dalton. Her arms were outstretched. Her long, bony fingers reached for him. They reached for the kid he once was.

Dalton remained seated. He didn't even flinch. He had truly let go of fear.

"Amen," he whispered.

Before the witch reached him, her body became ash. The ashes dissipated into the air within the office. Dalton waved what remained of her away with a simple flick of the wrist.

It is finished.

———

Well, everything is gonna be okay
He's going to wipe those tears away
And before the night is through
This is all going to make sense to you
Poor Old Lu – "Chance for the Chancers"

———

SKELETONS IN THE CHURCH CLOSET

Dalton awoke to the sound of knuckles rapping on the window against which his head leaned. Drool dripped down his chin. He wiped it away with one hand and turned his music down with the other.

Esther stood outside the car with her arms folded and a smirk on her face. Dalton rolled down the window and squinted up at her. The sun shone bright behind her as it made its way higher into the sky. Dalton thought she looked like an angel.

"Probably still asleep in the car, huh?"

Dalton made a face and shrugged his shoulders.

"I told you."

Esther put both hands on the door frame and leaned into the car. She kissed him. While her lips were still within range for a second kiss, she said, "Get out of the car. There's something I want to show you."

They walked through the front doors of the church. The glass of one of the doors had been shattered and a piece of plywood had been inserted to close it up.

"Didn't notice that before," Dalton said.

"Me either."

The foyer was impressive, but not quite as impressive as Dalton had imagined it, or dreamed it, or whatever it was when he had last been here.

"It's dusty," he said as his hand slid across a concession counter. Dust particles danced in the sunlight that shone through the glass entrance of the church.

They held hands as they walked the long hallway with all the doors. It seemed surreal to Dalton, walking down a hall that he had been in, but had never been in before.

"It's hot in here," he said. "Humid."

"Yeah," Esther said, "they should really turn on the air conditioners."

At the end of the hall they reached a big wooden door with a cross carved into it. The door had been pushed to one side of a mounted track.

"Through here," Esther said.

Dalton followed and found himself in a place he had not been, even in his mind.

"Cool. A fish tank."

He approached the large tank and grimaced. There was no water. The glass walls were green, thick with growth. Looking past the green, he noticed sagging fake foliage and scattered aquarium gravel.

"I think I see fish bones in the gravel."

"I'm sure you do," a voice that did not belong to Esther said.

Dalton whirled around. For a moment he tried to keep his composure, but the joy he experienced at seeing his new friend in real life overtook him.

"Abby!" He rushed to her and embraced her. "You're real!"

"I'm... real," she said. Her words sounded a tad strained. Dalton realized he was squeezing her entirely too tightly. He loosened his grip a bit.

"That's okay," she said with a chuckle. She wrapped her arms around his frame. "It's so good to finally meet you."

Dalton stopped hugging her, but left his hands on her shoulders. He looked into her face and said, "Abby, tell us, what actually happened last night?"

Abby looked at Esther, then back at Dalton.

"Let's take a walk."

The sanctuary was dark. It had the feel of an abandoned warehouse. It was so much larger than Dalton remembered it.

"No sign whatsoever of a three-headed dragon, huh?" he said, only half joking. The three of them walked down the center aisle toward the stage. Every chair was in its place. Every row was lined up perfectly. The massive curtain covered the stage.

Dalton looked up.

"No, Dalton," Esther scolded. "We are not going up there."

"Oh, come on!"

"I agree with Esther," Abby said, looking up too.

"Okay. Okay," Dalton said. "Probably just a bunch of bird nests up there anyway."

"Too soon," Abby said, but she was grinning. "Too soon."

They jumped up onto the stage and rolled under the curtain. Dalton half expected to see black ooze covering the floor of the stage. It was dark; it could be there.

Abby turned her phone's flashlight on.

The stage floor was clean, other than a thin layer of dust. Dalton and Esther pulled their phones out and turned their flashlights on as well. They explored the stage for a while, but quickly lost interest as there wasn't much to see. Dalton was upset that there were no instruments or band equipment anywhere. He noticed a thin line in the floor and assumed it was where the stage opened to reveal the baptismal. He was about to ask Abby about it when he noticed the old wooden preacher's podium. He walked over to it and used his phone's light to illuminate it.

"Holy crap!" he exclaimed.

"What?" Esther and Abby both asked in unison. They rushed over to look at the podium.

"It's..." Dalton was having a difficult time getting the words out. "It's... my dad's old podium. From when he was a pastor." He stood behind it, his hands placed on the sides as if he were about to deliver a sermon. His shoulders slumped.

"My dad used that podium every Sunday," Abby said. She moved to stand beside Dalton. "He told me one time that it was recovered from the ashes of the church that burned down on this property before this place was built." She put a hand on Dalton's back. "He said it represented beauty from ashes."

Dalton looked at her. Tears rolled down his cheeks.

"Your dad, I'm glad he thought that way."

"He wasn't a perfect man," she said, "but he always found a way to move forward."

"So, by the way you're talking," Esther interjected, very politely, as someone does when they are about to ask a delicate question, "I assume he's really gone."

Abby nodded her head. Her entire body drooped as if it was answering the question.

"Yes," she said. "Let's keep walking. I'll tell you how it happened."

They entered the hall leading to the Sunday-school classrooms. Not a word had been spoken since they left the sanctuary stage. Dalton thought it appropriate to maintain the silence until Abby was ready to break it. He was certain Esther thought similarly.

About halfway down the hall, Abby spoke up.

"There was a meeting," she began, "to determine if my father would remain the pastor." Her eyes looked down at her feet as she walked. Her pace was slow, which seemed appropriate for the weight of the story. "I had told him about Libby."

"Libby is your girlfriend?" Dalton asked.

"Yes." Abby looked up, and Dalton thought he saw the faintest smile form on her face. She looked down again and continued, "My dad didn't handle it well. Things were thrown. Awful words were said."

"Abby," Esther said, "I'm so sorry."

Abby shrugged her shoulders. "It's okay. I expected it. But what I didn't expect was how quickly he changed his tune. Not that he understood or even approved. He just... well, he started..."

"Operating out of love instead of fear?" Esther asked.

"Yeah," Abby said. "Exactly. He started leaning toward love, and that changed him. I don't think he anticipated how fast the change would happen, though. The church certainly didn't expect it, or like it."

"Thus, the meeting?" Dalton asked.

"Yes. The meeting."

They had reached the end of the hall. Dalton opened the door for Abby and Esther, who walked through. He began to follow, then paused for a moment to think about Kirk. Last night, this was where Dalton had seen him with a needle in his arm.

He walked through the door and closed it behind him.

Sun shone through the dome above the playground. It was so bright that Dalton's eyes hurt. He rubbed at them and noticed Abby and Esther do the same.

The ground under his feet was squishy.

Was it squishy in my dreams? He tried to remember.

They sat at a picnic table that was obviously meant for teachers to sit at while they supervised children playing on the equipment. Dalton sat beside Esther and put his index finger through one of the tiny holes that covered the green surface of the table.

Abby sat across from them. "All the staff and deacons and such met to decide my dad's fate. He wanted to start taking the church in a more... *progressive* direction."

"I assume they didn't like that," Dalton stated.

"No." Abby shoved four of her fingers into the small holes on the surface of the table, then yanked, for no reason. "One person in particular. His name was Victor." She said the name with malice. "He didn't like it so much that he pulled a gun out and started shooting."

"Oh my God!" Esther exclaimed. "Abby, I'm so sorry."

Abby didn't make eye contact. She just kept talking. "My dad died that day. He was rushed to the hospital, but he didn't make it. A few of the other pastors were shot, but they all survived, except for my friend Chad. His head was blown off." She took a deep breath and let it out. "Victor was arrested. The last time I talked to my dad was in the church reception area." She smiled, but it was accompanied by tears. "It was... a good talk."

Esther stood and walked around to Abby's side of the table to put an arm around her shoulders.

"After Dad passed," Abby continued, "I started having dreams. Vivid dreams. I dreamed of the meeting. There were demons involved. More people died every time. I couldn't stop thinking about why Victor did what he did. He'd known me from when I was born. He was kind to me. Then he killed my dad."

"Abby, it's not your fault," Dalton said. He felt he should have stayed silent, but the words jumped from his lips.

"Thank you," Abby said. "I know. But my brain keeps saying it anyway. I got to a very unhealthy place mentally. I stopped seeing Libby. As I told you before, the church closed down. It's been closed for over a year now. But I have my dad's keys, so I starting sneaking in. I don't know, I guess I thought if I could see Uncle Marvin one more time, he might say something to help me get over everything."

She looked around the room. Her gaze settled on the dome of light. She stared through it for a long time without talking.

"Can you tell me again about the day we met?" Esther asked eventually. "I'm sorry, but this is all still so confusing to me."

Abby shook her head as if trying to shake thoughts out of it.

"Yeah. No worries," she answered. "I was roaming the halls one day, acting all depressed and shit, when in walks a beautiful, dark-skinned, tattooed woman. I have to admit, I thought I was hallucinating at first."

"*I* was hallucinating!"

"You totally were. You kept saying you had a meeting with my dad. I told you that was impossible, but you insisted. So, I took you to his office and left you there. I didn't want to stay—going in his office is just too painful. I figured you were some random weirdo acting a part and trying to get a story for your murder podcast or something, but I was also worried for you. Something about you seemed sincere. So, just in case, I gave you my number."

"That was three months ago," Esther said.

"Yeah. I didn't hear from you again until last night. I was in the church when my phone buzzed. I got a text saying you were here. You called me Brittany."

"I thought I was texting Brittany!"

"Is there a real Brittany?" Dalton asked.

Abby shook her head. "Not that I know of."

"Thank God!" Dalton exclaimed.

"After the text message, I went to find Esther," Abby continued. "I found her in the sanctuary. She was running like she was being chased by something. There was nothing there. I thought about calling the cops and telling them a crazy person was trespassing, then I remembered that I was technically trespassing myself. When Esther ran toward me, a hooded figure appeared out of thin air. It was chasing her. In that moment, it was like my brain clicked over to a different operating system. I saw everything. It was all so... real."

Dalton nodded his head. Although he couldn't explain it other than labeling it "spiritual warfare," he understood exactly what she was talking about.

"I have a question," he said.

"Just one?" Esther joked.

"One pressing one. What about the women? I could have sworn women were being abused here, and that was the reason I was having dreams about this place." He buried his head in his hands. "I'm so dumb. I thought Uncle Marvin had come back somehow and was trying to tell me something. Trying to right a wrong."

Abby stood up quickly, as if something was wrong.

"Follow me," she said. She led them both to a closed door that opened into a maintenance closet they had all been in before. "I've just remembered something. We have one more stop on this tour."

Their positions were the same as the last time they had climbed the ladder. Abby led the way, with Esther in the middle and Dalton bringing up the rear. The climb was dark, and every bit as long as Dalton remembered it being. Abby pulled herself onto the hanging walkway and stood. Esther did the same, followed closely by Dalton. Both women pulled out their phones for light. Dalton's had died. He noticed that Abby and Esther both held tightly to the railing with their free hands as they made their way across the walkway, high above the sanctuary. He looked over the edge and, although he wasn't afraid of heights, he understood why people wouldn't want to come up here.

As if Abby knew what he was thinking, she said, "Not a lot of people ever came up here. Most people weren't allowed."

They passed the area where the bird's nest had been in their shared vision. Dalton shivered. He noticed goosebumps rise on Esther's arm to decorate her tattoos.

They made a sharp turn at the end of the walkway, onto another walkway.

"There's something at the end of this bridge I want to check out," Abby said. "When the beast had me, I saw someone here."

"Someone?" Dalton asked.

Abby didn't stop to explain. The walkway ended abruptly. The light from Abby's phone created a small circle of illumination on a blank wall. Dalton looked down and noticed they had reached one of the side walls of the sanctuary. Abby bent to inspect the area in front of her.

"What is it?" Esther asked.

"Hold my phone," Abby said. She handed it to Esther and then pulled a ring of keys out of her pocket. She inserted a key into the wall, into a keyhole that Dalton couldn't even see. He didn't even see the outline of a door.

"That doesn't make sense," Dalton said. "This should be an outer wall."

"Maybe this leads onto the roof?" Esther guessed.

The first key Abby tried didn't work, so she tried another, and then another. She had tried just about every key on the ring when one finally turned. She pushed the wall and it moved inward with a faint popping sound, like opened Tupperware.

The air around Dalton warmed. A putrid smell assaulted his nostrils. Esther shone both phone lights over Abby's shoulders.

"A secret room?" Dalton said. He used the inside of his arm to cover his nose, and breathed through his mouth. It barely helped.

"Oh my God!" Esther cried. She dropped the phone that had been held in her right hand and covered her mouth. The phone landed on the metal walkway with a thud. Its light shone up at the ceiling. Dalton picked it up and held it so that he could see into the room.

What he saw turned his stomach. There was a trash bag. A trash bag in the shape of a human being. Duct tape was wound around the bag, giving it form, much like a mummy's rags.

This is real, he told himself. *This is real.*

Esther leaned over the railing and threw up. Dalton secured her with one hand and held her hair back with his other, almost dropping the phone as he did so. Puke hit the sanctuary wall and cascaded down it like a grotesque waterfall, all the way to the sanctuary floor.

Abby took the phone from Dalton's hand.

"How did you find this place?" Dalton asked. Esther had finished vomiting. He held her steady within his arms. She looked up and wiped her mouth.

"When the beast had me," Abby said, "I saw someone here."

Dalton raised an eyebrow. "Was it who I hope it was?"

"Yes. It was Uncle Marvin. He was leaning against this very wall."

A moment of silence passed.

"Do you think that's for sure a body?" Esther asked, motioning inside the dark room.

"Only one way to find out," Abby answered.

She took a step into the room, walking delicately as if she was afraid she might fall through the floor. She approached the body bag and her fingers pulled at the area where a face might be. The black plastic stretched and lost color before it finally tore away to reveal the decaying face of a dead woman. Her skin was wrinkled. Her eyes sunken. The skin around her nose and mouth had completely disappeared, revealing red internal musculature. A set of yellow teeth almost glowed in the light from Abby's phone.

"That's her," Esther said. "I don't know how I know, but I know that's Brittany."

"I think you're right," Abby said solemnly. Her phone camera flashed, and as the bright light filled the room, Dalton's eyes widened at how many bodies he saw. There were at least a dozen of them.

"This picture is proof."

"I think we're done here," Esther said. "Let's get that picture to the cops."

"I agree," Abby said. She turned her back to the gruesome scene. "Let's get these women some justice."

————

Why does revival always get dressed for church?

Pastors search for it like it's a pot of gold at the end of a rainbow of promise.

God's children imagine it made of sugar and spice and worship services that last twice as long.

But revival is not a fairy tale.

We see it as an elusive unicorn. It more resembles a donkey that royalty rides while an orphan sits on a steed.

Revival is found in the mud. It's in the dirt under the fingernails of everyday people.

It is everyday, and it's rarely accompanied by a worship soundtrack.

It's a church function without a church building.

It's the body pulled from the rubble of an earthquake on the third day.

The immigrant, inmate, or outcast that is loved instead of labeled.

The office plant that gets watered by someone unknown.

A cup of cold water freely given.

When I was ready to walk on water while no one was watching, revival swallowed me up like a flood.

————

FINAL GIRL PASTOR

The cops had questions. The trio had agreed on their story—

Dalton had been feeling a touch nostalgic upon his return home and had wanted a tour of the church that had been built on top of his family's cemetery and old church. There was truth to the statement. Esther had contacted Abby and asked if she and Dalton could be shown around. Abby had assumed it was okay because she still had keys to the place. While exploring, Abby had noticed a keyhole in the wall that she had never seen before. It struck her as odd, since she knew just about everything there was to know about the building.

"Pastors' kids know the church better than anyone," she told the police.

She had decided to try all the keys on her father's keyring. One opened a door to a hidden room and they had found the bodies.

The cops believed them. The story was true, from a certain point of view.

Months passed. Rumors about the bodies found within the abandoned mega-church swirled. Hillside was once again a church everyone was talking about, and not just the locals. There were podcasts and YouTube videos. Eventually, a documentary was released on one of the big streaming services. The police cracked the case. The murderer was charged with multiple counts of homicide dating back over a decade. He was not arrested, however, because he had *already* been arrested. The man dubbed the Congregation Killer by the media was a longtime member of the church, and also a deacon. His name was Victor, and he had been arrested for murdering his senior pastor and worship leader a year ago. It turned out that Victor was more than just an angry man with a gun. He was a bona fide serial killer. His modus operandi was torturing and killing women in the church who presumed to think they belonged in leadership or positions of authority that rightfully belonged to men. Almost all his victims were congregants of Hillside Church. Because of the church's closure, many called it a miracle that the bodies of the women had even been found.

"And the saddest part is," Dalton said to James, keeping his voice low as he didn't want the children to overhear, "while the church was still operating, they didn't even notice the women were missing. They just assumed they had all become offended and left."

James shook his head. He flipped a final burger and then shut the lid of the grill. Smoke enveloped his head. He set down the spatula, took his glasses off, and rubbed them clean with the bottom of his polo shirt.

"That's awful," he said as he put his glasses back on. "The church in general has a long way to go when it comes to how it treats women." He took a sip of his beer.

"Amen to that," Patricia said.

She walked over to her boys and stood between them. Her hair was short and almost all gray. She wore glasses that weren't that different than the ones James wore. White capri pants showed off her calves and a blue and white top completed her outfit. She put one arm around each of her children's shoulders and watched the kids playing in the back yard.

Esther approached and passed Dalton a can of Dr Pepper. He cracked it open and took a sip.

"What are we talking about?" Esther asked.

"Change." Patricia said.

"I'll drink to that," Esther said, holding up her beer bottle.

"To change," James said with his bottle raised.

"Hear, hear!" Dalton exclaimed with his can of soda lifted high.

They drank and continued to watch the children play. When a little time had passed, Esther looked at Dalton and asked, "Should we tell them?"

"Should you tell us what?" James inquired.

"Whatever it is, you tell your mother *now*!" Patricia demanded.

Dalton smiled. He hesitated just long enough to make sure his mother was at her wits' end with worry.

"We should tell them."

"You're getting married!"

The voice belonged to James' wife. She held a two-year-old in her arms. Her name was Brianna, but everyone called her Bri. She and James had met at UAB hospital, where James had done his residency, and where she was an oncologist. She leaned on James and nodded her head. "Yup, I can see it in your eyes. It's marriage."

"No," Dalton answered. "We're actually... *already* married."

"What!" Patricia bellowed. She slapped her son on the shoulder, hard. "Why weren't we invited?"

"Hey!" Dalton yelled while backing away from his mom. "Chill. We got married a few weeks ago at the courthouse. We thought we would surprise you with the news when we came for our visit."

"I'm so sorry, Patricia," Esther said. She covered her heart with her hands. "We just felt at over forty years old, a courthouse wedding was better for everybody. More our style, too. My shop is close to the courthouse. I got off work and walked right to my wedding."

Patricia beamed. "Don't you worry about it, dear. I'm just happy the two of you are happy."

"Well, Mom, you're gonna be even happier when we tell you the *real* news."

"Oh my God!" Patricia said. "Don't tell me... Another grandkid?"

Dalton and Esther locked hands.

"Another grandkid," Dalton said with a grin on his face.

"We've decided to adopt!" Esther announced.

Everyone cheered. Patricia cried. James shook Dalton's hand, then Dalton pulled him in for a hug. Bri hugged Esther with her free arm. Dalton and James pulled their mother in for an embrace. Esther cried. Bri squeezed her tighter. The baby was squished between them. Soon they all had their arms around each other in a big group hug.

"Dad!" a toddler's voice shouted. "Dad!"

James pulled away from the group and looked at his son. "Yes, Andrew? Sorry. We are just happy because Uncle Dalton and Aunt Esther are going to be adopting a kid. You're going to have a new cousin. Isn't that wonderful?"

The boy looked up at his dad with big brown eyes and said, "That's awesome!"

Everyone smiled at him. His brother and little sister joined him.

"But Dad..." He pointed at the grill. White smoke billowed out of it. "I think the burgers are burning."

***

Abby fluffed the pillows on her couch.

"What are you doing?" Libby asked. "Why are you fluffing pillows?"

"I don't know!" Abby answered. "I just need everything to be perfect."

"I highly doubt anyone that shows up is going to be concerned with the level at which our pillows are fluffed."

A pillow struck Libby in the face.

"That's for making me feel ridiculous."

Libby picked the pillow up off the floor and fluffed it, then placed it gently on the couch. "There," she said, "how do you feel now?"

"Better."

"But not perfect?"

"No," Abby admitted. "I would feel a whole lot better if I knew anyone was gonna show up."

"Abby. We had plenty of people respond. On Instagram and Facebook. At least one person is going to show up for this Bible study."

"And if they don't?" Abby asked sarcastically.

Libby put her arms around her girlfriend. "What is it you always say? Where two or more are gathered..."

"God is among them."

"We are two," Libby said. She touched the tip of Abby's nose. "One."

Abby's put a finger to the tip of her girlfriend's nose. "Two," she said.

"God is already here. You made me believe that."

Abby collapsed into Libby's arms.

"Thank you. It's just..." She let out a deep breath. A lot of her stress left her body with the exhalation. "I really want this home church to work. I still don't know if anyone will show up to the house of a female pastor. Much less a *gay* female pastor."

"If they don't," Libby said, "then it's their loss. And also, we'll have all the chips and dip to ourselves."

"Dear Lord, we bought too much French onion dip." Abby pulled away and walked over to a table full of snacks. "Just look at that bowl of dip!"

"I beg to differ," Libby said. "If no one shows up I'll end up eating that entire bowl myself." She picked up a chip and used it like a spoon, shoveling a far too large amount of dip onto it. The chip should have broken under its weight, but before it had a chance, Libby shoved it into her mouth and chewed with her mouth open.

"Eww!" Abby screeched. "You're basically chewing nothing but onion dip!"

"*Mmmm!*" Libby picked up another chip and scooped up an amount of dip that exceeded the amount her last chip had held. She moved it toward Abby's mouth, like a parent pretending a spoonful of mashed potatoes was an airplane coming in for a landing. "You want some dip?"

The doorbell rang. Libby dropped the chip. It plopped into the bowl of dip.

"Someone's here!" Abby exclaimed.

She ran to open the door. Just before she opened it, she looked at Libby.

"You got this, pastor," Libby said.

Abby opened the door.

"Sarah! I'm so glad you could make it."

Sarah was the younger sister of Chad, Abby's best friend who had died on the same day as her father.

"Come on in," Abby said. "You're the first one here."

Before Sarah had even reached the snack table, the doorbell rang again.

"Xavier! So cool of you to come. Come on in."

The pattern continued until Abby wasn't sure they had bought enough dip. When it seemed that everyone had arrived and had had enough to eat, the group sat in the living room, ready to listen to Abby speak. The house now technically belonged to her, but in her heart she would always be living rent free in her parents' house. A framed photo of the three of them hung above the fireplace—the same photo that had once hung in the dining room, which she had moved to the living room the day before. She wanted her dad to see her lead her first service.

She looked around the room. It was packed with people. People who loved her. People that weren't afraid of who she was. She looked up at the photo of her parents. She knew it was impossible, but it almost looked like their smiles were growing.

After what I've been through, she thought, *I'm not sure that's impossible.*

"Thank you all so much for coming," she began. "I can't tell you how much it means to me that—"

The doorbell rang. Abby watched as Libby went to answer the door. Abby had just started to explain how she had always felt called by God to be a minister when Libby walked back into the room with four additional people, who all waved discreetly and smiled at Abby. They leaned against the back wall of the living room because there were no more available seats.

Abby's train of thought was derailed at the sight of the new people. Of course she had sent them an invite, but she had never expected them to actually show up. Sending them an invitation had been more a way for her to keep them in the loop. They had *asked* to be kept in the loop. Sure, she had thought that maybe James and Bri would be able to make it, but Dalton and Esther lived in Florida. She had assumed there was no way. But there they sat: James, Bri, Esther and Dalton. They were all here. They were at church.

Dalton looked a bit uncomfortable. His arms were crossed and his eyes darted around the room as if he was looking for something. Maybe a demon? Or a witch demon?

No, Abby thought. *He's moved past all that.*

As Dalton's eyes met Abby's, he seemed to relax. She grinned at him. He smiled back and gave her a thumbs up.

"You've got this," he mouthed, "pastor."

Abby nodded.

"I've always felt called by God."

THE END

Content warnings: Spiritual abuse. Physical abuse. Sexual abuse including rape. Child abuse. Murder. Torture. Homophobia. Gun violence. Attempted suicide.

Acknowledgments

Thank you to my God.

Thank you to my wife and kids.

Thank you to my little brother.

Thank you to Billy Atchison and Carl Jones.

Amen.

This is a work of fiction. I shouldn't have to explain that. Names, characters, business, events, and incidents are the products of the author's imagination. Any resemblance to actual persons, living or dead, or actual events is purely coincidental. If this book offends you, pray about it.

Please remember to leave a review!
Contact: starfold7@gmail.com
Find me on Instagram @BIBLEBELTHORROR
Check out Andrew's other books wherever books are sold!

About the Author

Andrew is a former pastor that now tells horror stories. His Bible Belt Horror series is a collection of books that reflect the mental struggles his mind dealt with as it navigated church culture.